PRAISE FO

"Funny, sexy, perfection. Equal p:
—*Adriane 1*

"The THAT MAN series keeps getting better and better, funnier and sexier. Bravo, Nelle! No wonder this series is a runaway success!"
—*Arianne Richmonde, USA Today Bestselling Author*

"Blake Burns . . . the most funny and charming boyfriend next to Andrew Parrish and Drew Evans"

—*Bedtime Reads*

"THAT MAN has everything readers could want. A funny and sexy read. Phenomenal!"

—*The Fairest of All Book Reviews*

"Not only is Blakemeister back, but he's on fire!!"
—*A is For Alpha, B is for Books Blog*

"Be prepared for another hot, sexy, and humorous read."
—*Love Between the Sheets Book Blog*

"The chemistry between Blake and Jennifer is amazing! I felt like I was there with them."

—*SubClub Books*

"Is it possible to love Blake even more than I did? A resounding YES!
—*Goodreads Reviewer*

"Nelle L'Amour's writing is the perfect mixture of sexy dialogue, relatable characters, and laugh out-loud moments. Get ready to fall in love with THAT MAN all over again."

—*Vanessa Booke, USA Today Bestselling Author*

"Packed with more intense romance and suspense that will just blow your head into the water. Amazing!"

—*Whispered Thoughts Book Blog*

BOOKS BY NELLE L'AMOUR

Unforgettable
Unforgettable Book 1
Unforgettable Book 2
Unforgettable Book 3

Alpha Billionaire Duet
TRAINWRECK 1
TRAINWRECK 2

A Standalone Romantic Comedy
Baby Daddy

An OTT Insta-love Standalone
The Big O

THAT MAN Series
THAT MAN 1
THAT MAN 2
THAT MAN 3
THAT MAN 4
THAT MAN 5
THAT MAN 6

Gloria
Gloria's Secret
Gloria's Revenge
Gloria's Forever

An Erotic Love Story
Undying Love
Endless Love

Writing as E.L. Sarnoff
DEWITCHED: The Untold Story of the Evil Queen
UNHITCHED: The Untold Story of the Evil Queen 2

Boxed Sets
THAT MAN TRILOGY
THAT MAN: THE WEDDING STORY
Unforgettable: The Complete Series
Gloria's Secret: The Trilogy
Seduced by the Park Avenue Billionaire
Naughty Nelle

THAT MAN 6

THAT
MAN
₆

NELLE L'AMOUR

To join my mailing list for new releases, sales, and giveaways, please sign up here:
NEWSLETTER: nellelamour.com/newsletter

NICHOLS CANYON PRESS
Los Angeles, CA USA

THAT MAN 6

Cover by Arijana Karčic/Cover It! Designs
Proofreading by: Mary Jo Toth
Formatting by BB eBooks

For all of my Belles who wanted more of scorchin' hot Blake Burns.

In life, the only thing you can expect is the unexpected.

—Joan Rivers

THAT MAN 6

Chapter 1

Jennifer

DAY ONE

"**B**lake, are we there yet?"

My gorgeous husband chortles. "Jeez, tiger, you sound like one of our kids." Wearing aviator sunglasses and a headset, he turns to give me a saucy grin.

"Oh my God, Blake! Get your eyes back on the dashboard."

"Instrument panel," he corrects. Whatever it's called, it's a dizzying array of monitors and dials. Thank goodness, he does as I've asked.

"Chill, baby. I've got this. According to the GPS, we'll be landing in two hours."

What! Two hours! I don't think I can take more of this. Besides being somewhat claustrophobic, I'm not a great flyer. Trust me, being in this small, one-engine plane hasn't been a picnic. Not for a minute! Butterflies flit around my stomach. A swarm. The sooner we get there the better.

I don't know what possessed my husband to take up flying and become a certified pilot. Wasn't flying me into the stratosphere with his insatiable cock enough? The bigger question is what possessed me to let him fly us to the Maldives for our tenth anniversary and agree to be his co-pilot? The answer to the first question: he was out of his mind. The answer to the second: I was out of *my* mind!

To celebrate our special anniversary, Blake wanted to go to a place where we could relax and get away from our everyday craziness. We don't live an ordinary life. It's one of glamour, glitz, and hard work. Every minute is scheduled. He's the high-powered head of Conquest Broadcasting while I'm in charge of their children's network, Peanuts. Besides our all-consuming jobs, which require long hours, countless meetings, black-tie events, and out-of-town business trips, we're the parents of two rambunctious children—Leo, age 8, and Maeve, almost 5. We're constantly juggling our careers and parenthood. Somehow, we've found the time to take the kids to school, go to all of Leo's Little League games and Maeve's ballet recitals, as well as spend quality time together as a family that includes Friday night Shabbat dinners with his entire family and my parents, weekends at local attractions like the zoo and museums, plus fun-filled vacations to Disneyworld, New York City, Sun Valley, and Europe. Blake and I have also managed one other thing: to spend quality time in our bedroom. While we have a fantastic marriage that's rooted in equality, mutual respect, and our deep-seated love for one another, it's where Blake exerts his control and I totally lose it. And love every minute.

To be honest, I would have been perfectly happy staying home—there's no place else I'd rather be than with my two amazing kids—but Blake wanted to fly to an island. To have some special alone time together just for us. He came up with the bright idea while fucking me over his desk. It's nice that we work in the same building and that he runs the company and makes the rules. Or bends them.

There's a boatload of islands he could have flown us to. Some almost in our backyard like Catalina or those outside San Diego. But, no, Mr. Adventurer had to choose one that was almost 10,000 miles away from our house in Santa Monica. Twenty hours of flying time. You can do the math—we've been in the air for eighteen long hours. An eternity!

It's actually been a two-fold trip. On the first leg, we flew on a glamorous chartered Gulfstream 650 that felt much like being in the presidential suite of The Four Seasons with its sleek leather and teak furnishings, state-of-the art kitchen, and steam-shower bathroom. Blake co-piloted the plane for several hours while I slept under the covers of a yummy Egyptian cotton comforter in a comfy bed.

That plane, however, could only take us as far as Sri Lanka. There we switched planes. Or more precisely, we traded our deluxe jet in for this turbo prop plane, one that could land on the small, narrow runway of the private island we're staying on.

The prop plane is nothing like the luxurious, spacious Gulfstream. It only has six seats, including ours, and we're lucky it has a toilet . . . a porta-potty of sorts. Ugh! Blake brought so much luggage along that it takes up almost all the space of the aircraft. So, I'm stuck in the cockpit serving as his co-pilot.

Not a good flyer to begin with, I've been in freakout mode ever since we took off from the airport. Blake, in contrast, has been like a kid on an amusement park ride. Starting with a "whoo hoo" as we took off.

"Tiger, seriously. Just relax and enjoy the view."

Sitting next to him, I force myself to look out the window and cast my eyes down, avoiding the rotating propeller, which adds to my unease. Ten thousand feet up in the air, I can see a lush island below—tops of palm trees and verdant terrain surrounded on all sides by miles of the green-blue Indian Ocean. All crystal-clear thanks to my recent Lasik surgery, something Blake convinced me to have because I was forever losing my eyeglasses. With no buildings, vehicles, or roads in sight, the island seems to be deserted. Unfortunately, the breathtaking view does little to calm my nerves. My stomach bunches. I feel queasy.

Suddenly, a rumble thunders in my ears. I whip my head around and face Blake.

"Fuck!" he shouts out, terror flickering on his face.

"What's going on, Blake?" My voice is in a panic.

"There's something wrong with the engine."

"Oh my God! Are you serious?"

"Yes!"

Hardly the answer I want to hear. The engine continues to rumble. My heart leaps into my throat. It's beating at a gazillion miles an hour.

"Oh my God," I repeat, my voice now frantic.

"Put on your life jacket!"

I fumble for the yellow vest that's stored under my seat. Slipping it over my head, it takes me two tries to fasten it because my hands are shaking so much. I pull down on the tabs to inflate it.

"Blake, what about you?"

"I can't let go of the control wheel."

Pushing it forward, he clutches the U-shaped handles so tightly his knuckles turn white. He curses again as the plane begins to wobble. My stomach lurches. I may throw up. I clamp my mouth shut, biting hard on my bottom lip, so I don't.

"See if you can radio someone."

In my panicked state I push the emergency call button. "Blake, all I get is static."

"Shit. Try the satellite phone."

Even more panicked, I do again as I'm asked. *Nada!* "Blake, I still can't get through." I turn to look at my husband. I've never seen a more intense expression on his face. His jaw is tight, his lips pinched, his eyes unblinking. Fear, like none other, claws at me.

I look out the window again. "Blake, what's that liquid pouring out of the wing?"

"What!" His eyes train on the fuel gauge. "Shit! We're leaking fuel!"

"Oh my God!" Our situation has just gone from bad to worse. Way worse! We're not going to last in the air!

"Blake, what are we going to do?" I spit out the words, panic gripping my insides.

"Tiger, hold on. I'm going to attempt to land this baby."

Hold on to what? The only thing I want to hold on to is my life. A nauseating mixture of terror, regret, and sorrow swishes through my veins. We're going to die! Crash into the shark-infested water and drown. Or crash land on some remote island and die in a fiery explosion. Anyway I look at it, our lives are over. And I'll never see my treasured family again. Our two beautiful children . . . Our beloved parents . . . His precious grandma . . . Her big-hearted husband Luigi . . . Or all our wonderful friends . . . Libby, Chaz, Jaime, Gloria, and so many others.

"Blake, I'm so scared!" I choke out.

"Be brave, my tiger!"

I've had to be Blake's brave tiger many times in my life, but this isn't one of them. I start to sob as the wobbly plane begins to lose altitude.

"Close your eyes, baby!" Blake orders, his voice commanding and intense.

With tears streaming, I do as he asks, squeezing my eyes shut. So tightly they hurt. The truth is, I don't want to see our ugly demise.

"C'mon, c'mon, c'mon," I hear Blake mumble. The plane shakes violently. A warning siren sounds. My stomach lurches again as we plummet. I hold my breath and lose all sense of time. Then suddenly, a tumultuous thud makes my stomach somersault and my heart do cartwheels.

All I can hear are ear-splitting screams. The screams are mine, and as they pierce the air, I know they won't save us.

Chapter 2

Blake

"YES!" Holy shit! I've successfully landed this aircraft. In one piece! My heart's still racing, my hands glued to the controls, my feet pressed tight on the brakes as the plane comes to a juddering halt. My wife's sobs fill the cockpit.

Relaxing my hands, I blow out a hot breath and release some of my pent-up tension. My muscles slowly unclench one vertebra at a time. I swivel toward my tiger.

"Jen, baby, are you okay?"

I don't think she can hear me. Or see me with her eyes squeezed shut.

Letting go of the gear, I tear off my headset and lift my sunglasses on top of my head. Then I cup my wife's heaving shoulders and gently turn her to face me. She slowly opens her watering eyes and blinks them several times as if she's seeing a mirage. Her pale as a ghost face is streaked with tears that keep falling, and her glossed lips are trembling. She looks like she just lost her best friend in the world. The truth: she almost did. Even with countless hours of flight training, I wasn't prepared for an emergency. What got me through was an elixir of tunnel vision and adrenaline. On a wing and a prayer, I kept praying that we wouldn't crash land.

Kissing the top of her head, I brush away her tears with my thumbs. "Baby, it's okay. We made it."

My words seem to offer her no comfort. She sobs. I wipe away more tears. "Shh, baby. *We're* okay."

"Oh, Blake," she finally splutters. "I was so scared. I thought for sure we were going to die."

"Nah, landing this baby was a piece of cake." Mentally, I give myself the prize for best liar in the world. I was scared shitless too. Close to flipping out. I look deep into her glistening green eyes, the eyes I fell in love with after a blindfolded kiss that changed my life forever. "C'mon baby, you know I'm *That Man*. Your superhero. I'd never let anything happen to you."

"I'd even kill for you," I say to myself. And I did. Over ten years ago, I saved her from a murderous rapist. A deranged game show producer who blamed her for losing his job with the network. And who'd uncannily almost raped her while she was in college. I vowed to her then that I'd always be there for her. Be *that* man who would take care of her and protect her. *That* man who would love her until death do us part. A shiver skitters down my spine at the thought of how close we just came to the end of our journey together.

The chill dissipates with relief at the thought that we survived and that I can go on loving her.

"Tiger, tell me you're okay."

Her sobs subsiding, she nods.

I cradle her tear-stained face. "Baby, I need to hear words."

"Blake, I'm okay." Her voice is a raspy whisper. "I love you so much."

My eyes burn into hers. "I love you more."

A faint smile plays on her kissable lips. "If more is possible."

Love for this woman fills my every pore. Still holding her beautiful face in my hands, my lips press down on hers, sucking and gnawing them. The last time I kissed her like this was in Los Angeles before we boarded the Gulfstream at Van Nuys Airport. Almost twenty-four hours ago. I've missed these sweet lips. I kiss her like there's no tomorrow, and knowing how close we came to that reality, she succumbs to my mouth and my tongue as it dances with hers. After several delicious minutes, I break it. She holds me in her gaze.

"Blake, what are we going to do?"

My eyes for the first time take in our surroundings. We've landed on the beach of some tropical island. The sugar-white sand glistens, the turquoise ocean sparkles, and in the distance, tall palm trees lick the sky. The only thing that's missing from this paradise is a Ritz

Carlton. Or a Four Seasons.

"We're going to start celebrating our ten-year anniversary. Consider this a second honeymoon."

"But, Blake, we need to focus on getting off this island." Her eyes take in our surroundings. "Do you think anyone lives here?"

"I think this would be a great place to build a casino."

"What are you saying, Blake?"

"Build it and they will come."

"Meaning . . ."

"Population: Two." I hold up two fingers, like a peace symbol. "It's you and me, baby."

Despair washes over my tiger's face. She looks on the verge of tears again.

"Don't worry, baby, someone will find us." I kiss her again, wanting to believe my own words.

Chapter 3

Jennifer

Dressed in a Conquest Broadcasting sweatshirt, a long-sleeved blouse, and jeans, I feel sweat pouring down my back as Blake unloads the last pieces of luggage from the plane. Mid afternoon, it must be close to ninety degrees. The sun is blazing and the air is humid.

I count the Louis Vuitton bags. A dozen. Oh, those are just his. My high maintenance, metrosexual husband must have brought along his entire wardrobe plus filled up three satchels with his sunglass collection, cigars, and grooming products. Taking my husband to a beauty supply store is like taking a kid to a toy store.

Blake chucks my two bags onto the sand along with a small compact blue valise I don't recognize and then jumps out of the plane. I smile at my "designer" bags, thoughtful gifts from my husband last Christmas—one a SpongeBob SquarePants roller bag filled with my wardrobe for a tropical vacation and the other, a matching duffle filled with necessities like deodorant, shampoo and conditioner, my makeup, sunscreen, bug repellent, and of course, Band-Aids and other first-aid stuff given my accident proneness. "Calamity Jen" as my best friend Libby aptly nicknamed me.

Sweat beads on Blake's forehead as he ambles toward me. "Jesus, this place feels like the steam room at Equinox. I'm hot as hell."

He *is* as hot as hell. I drink him in. At almost forty-years old, he's still as breathtaking as ever. Sexy as sin. Lean and buff in his ripped jeans and a T-shirt. Age has only made him more handsome with the fine lines webbing around the corners his twinkling sapphire eyes, giving him character and depth. Just like his father, he still has a full head of glorious hair, but where they differ is that Blake has yet to go gray. Not even a strand.

He rakes his hand through his dark tousled locks. "Aren't you hot, babe?"

"Yes, I'm really hot." My damp clothes are clinging to me.

Mischief flickers in his eyes. "Yeah, you look really hot."

Sweating, I feel myself heat further at his innuendo. Tingle all over.

"C'mon, lets get undressed and cool off."

He starts to disrobe, pulling his T-shirt over his head. I marvel at his chiseled chest, his broad pecs, and those washboard abs maintained by his personal trainer.

I'm seriously salivating as if it's the first time I've seen his museum-worthy sculpted body. With my index finger, I brush away the bit of spittle from the corner of my lips as a hot pool of wetness gathers between my legs and my skin prickles with need. Maybe after this insufferable journey, I need to cool off another way. Blake's gleaming eyes stay on me. Tossing his shirt onto the sand, he shoots me a smirk. After almost ten years of marriage, Blake can read my mind. And my dirty thoughts.

As he kicks off his Italian loafers and undoes his jeans, I begin to undress, taking off my sweatshirt and then unbuttoning my damp, clingy blouse. Blake's eyes stay on me as my breasts come into view. My perfect tits, he likes to call them, and just the thought of him tweaking my nipples sends another rush of sparks to my core.

Blake, as usual, has gone commando. The sight of his magnificent cock and that perfect pelvic-V makes me fumble with the button of my jeans. He's getting enormous satisfaction watching me. In more ways than one.

He moves in closer to me. "Here, let me help you." He easily unbuttons my jeans with his deft fingers as I step out of my Vans. With a whoosh, he slides down the zipper and then shoves down the skinny denims. So aroused, I clumsily step out of them. I'm left wearing just a pink lace thong.

His dazzling, dimpled smile stretches across his face as he zeroes in on the scanty undergarment. "Those are very pretty, baby, but honestly, I'd much rather see your pretty pink pussy." On my next heartbeat, he rips them off.

My breath hitches in my throat. "Blake, we should put on some sunscreen and bathing suits. Maybe set things up. Try to call for help."

"The aircraft radio still isn't working. Nor is the satellite phone."

"What about your cell?"

"Baby, I've already tried it. I don't think they have Verizon here."

My heart sinks. Again the thought of getting off this island invades my head.

Before I can despair, he scoops me up into his arms. "Come on baby, let's cool off."

Five minutes later, I'm floating in the most beautiful water I've ever known.

Chapter 4

Blake

Our swim in the ocean has stirred my appetite. It's also stirred something else. Mr. Burns, my always-hungry-for-my-wife cock. You'd think I couldn't get hard given how seriously fucked up our situation is, but Mr. Burns has a mind of his own. He did not enjoy being holed up in that cockpit. Not one bit. The only downside of being a pilot—besides crashing—is that you can't have any fun in the mile-high club while flying.

Jen's now in my arms, her toned legs and arms wrapped around me, the buoyancy of the calm, warm water holding her up. It's a little over waist-deep and feels like a bath.

"Baby, I'm scared. What if no one finds us?"

"Stop worrying." I brush a loose wet curl behind her ear. "When my father doesn't hear from me around the time we were supposed to arrive at the hotel, he'll have the entire military looking for us."

"My father will have a coronary."

"Baby, he won't. Your father is made of steel."

"Then, my mother will."

"Nah, baby. She's stronger than you think." I think back to the time Jen had her emergency surgery and how her mother was there for her. Solid as a rock. "What's it going to take for you to stop worrying?"

"I don't know."

"I do. We're on our second honeymoon. It's going to take a good fucking."

As a gentle wave lifts us up, I lower my hand into the water and curl my fingers around the base of my cock. On my next breath, I plunge it into her. She lets out a gasp and digs her fingers into my shoulders. My hands move to her firm buttocks, gripping them tightly.

"Ride me, baby!" I breathe against her neck.

"Oh God, Blake!" I'm already lifting her up and down my shaft. Her supple breasts grazing my chest, she meets my thrusts, arching her neck back, as the sun begins to set behind us. Bursting with need from the twenty-hour trip, I know I'm not going to last long. Nor is she. I finger her clit under the water, strumming her hypersensitive bundle of nerves, as she continues to buck me. The warm water laps against us, creating little splashes of erotic bliss as I kiss her silky wet skin, savoring the sweetness and saltiness. My other hand moves to her dangling ponytail, and I tug it hard as her muscles convulse around my ready to combust cock. Whimpering, she cries out my name and comes as rapidly as I do. Oh, yeah! Mr. Burns is as happy as a clam.

It's just what she needed. And I needed to get through this day.

Chapter 5

Jennifer

"I'm starving," says Blake as we head back to the beach. His arm is wrapped around me, thankfully as my legs are like Jell-O after our romp in the ocean. I have to admit he was right. It was exactly what I needed to calm down.

"Me too," I reply. Dusk is approaching. The sun's sinking into the horizon as a breeze from the sea kicks up. I haven't eaten for hours.

"What time is it?" I ask.

Blake glances down at his waterproof Rolex. "I'm trying to figure it out. My watch is still set to LA time. It's seven-thirty in the morning there."

I roll my eyes. "It's not too hard to figure out. There's a twelve-hour time difference."

"How do you know that?"

"I did research. So, I'd know what time to FaceTime the kids." My worry-free reprieve is fleeting. A bolt of sadness sweeps through me at the thought that I may never see them again. Or hear their sweet voices.

I force optimism back into my ventricles as Blake knits his brows. "So that means it's seven-thirty p.m. here." He gives me an affectionate squeeze. "That's one of the reasons I married you, tiger. Because you're so smart."

Just not smart enough to talk him out of flying lessons or to say no to this trip. Where were my brains then? What was I thinking?

By the time we reach our stuff, we're more or less dried off. I unzip my duffle and fish for my hairbrush. Finding it, I undo my ponytail, run the bristles through my hair, and then tie it up again. Then, I unzip my other bag and put on a pretty floral sundress. One of the many Libby's brother, hot fashion designer Chaz, gave me for our trip. The two of them are like family to me. It's partly because of the Truth or Dare game they put me through that I fell in love with Blake.

"That dress looks pretty on you, baby," comments my husband as he slips on a pair of board shorts. "But truthfully, I can't wait to take it off."

I feel my cheeks flush at his words. After ten years of marriage, he still knows how to push all my buttons. To make me lust for him.

As I zip up my bags, he ties his trunks. "Hey babe, did you bring along any bras?"

"Yes, why?"

"I'm going to need them to make a fire."

"You're going to burn my bras?"

"Yeah," he replies with a fiendish grin. "You don't need them. I'll buy you some new ones."

Yeah, right . . . at the local Gloria's Secret. Time to ask him the burning question. "You know how to make a fire?" My born-with-a-silver-spoon-in-his-mouth husband doesn't even know how to turn on the burner on our stove.

"Yup, Scout's Honor." He lifts his right hand and gives me the three-finger Scout salute.

I mentally roll my eyes again. For over ten years, I've heard my husband use this phrase. I've never believed for a nano-second that Blake was a Boy Scout, and he's never proven it to me.

Keeping his right hand lifted, he digs the other into a pocket and recites the Boy Scout motto. "Be prepared. Look what I've got." Grinning, he holds up the gold lighter that once belonged to his late grandpa.

Okay, so there's hope for a fire. Somehow, I couldn't imagine Blake scratching two sticks together like a caveman.

"Babe, I'm going to go back to the plane and see if there's anything left to eat and drink. Then, I'm going to set up our deluxe accommodations. While I'm doing that, why don't you take a walk along the beach and look for some wood." He grins again. "Don't talk to any strangers."

"Very funny." I snort with sarcasm. How my husband can have such a sense of humor when we're in survival mode is beyond me. Retrieving a tote bag from my suitcase, I go on my way while Blake heads back to the plane.

A half-hour later, we meet up. I'm carrying a tote full of sticks and bark I found along the beach. Probably remnants of tropical storms. I also collected some pretty seashells we can put around the fire. It looks like Blake's been busy. My eyes grow as round as saucers.

"Oh my God, Blake. What's this?" I stare at the rubber and nylon construct. It resembles an oversized pup tent with its inflatable bright yellow mattress and orange V-shaped canopy.

"It's the life raft. I blew it up with the canister of gas it came with."

"Wow! Impressive." That's what must have been in that mysterious blue valise.

"We'll sleep in it tonight." He admires his creation. "I also scored in the food department."

I set my heavy tote down as he crawls into the tent. He re-emerges, holding a Whole Foods bag.

"Good news, baby. There was some food leftover. And enough bottled waters to last a couple weeks." While the thought of being marooned on this island for more than twenty-four hours sends a chill down my spine, I look down at the assortment he's begun to spread out on a blanket outside the tent. I bend down to help him.

Not that we really needed it on the Gulfstream with

its gourmet cuisine and full bar, Blake's Jewish mother stocked up the deluxe jet with lots of good food and healthy snacks. Slipping my hand into the brown paper bag, I lift out a large plastic container. My heart warms and I can't help but smile.

"Look, Blake! Your grandma made us some matzo ball soup."

Blake's face lights up too. "And guess what baby, it's Friday. Shabbat! We'll make this our Shabbat dinner."

A hoard of memories and emotions bombard me. That first Shabbat at Blake's house where I lit the candles and ate matzo ball soup for the first time with Blake's lustful eyes on me. Mentally undressing me. And, the afternoon his oversexed grandma taught me how to make the doughy balls, which I sensuously fed to Blake before he fucked me senseless on the kitchen floor. And all the fun family Shabbat dinners since then with Blake's wonderful family, my parents, and our children. The smile on my face fades as sadness washes over me. Maybe this will be my last Shabbat with Blake. And I'll never see our family again. I fight back tears.

"What's the matter, baby?" he asks.

Reaching back into the bag, I spread out some plastic plates and utensils. "I was just thinking."

"About what?"

"Us . . . our family. You know . . ." My voice trails

off.

Blake tenderly tilts up my chin. "C'mon, baby. Let's be optimistic and enjoy the moment."

"Did you try the satellite phone again?"

"Yeah. It's dead. I couldn't get a signal. Maybe the plane had an electrical outage."

Disappointed, I press my lips thin while Blake digs his hand into a much smaller paper bag.

"Cheer up! Look what else I found!" He holds it up. A bottle of Dom Perignon. Wasting no time, he removes the foil and loosens the wire cage. My eyes train on his magnificent forearms, flexing as he twists and turns the cork. Then . . . POP!

He sets the bottle down and retrieves two plastic flutes from the brown bag. I watch as he pours the bubbly into them. He lifts his glass and proposes a toast.

"L'Chaim."

To life. I brush my flute against his before taking a sip. Never before have these two words meant more to me.

Thanks to Blake's mother and his grandma, our makeshift Shabbat meal is delicious. In addition to the matzo ball soup which Blake heated up by placing the container close to the campfire, we devour mouth-watering rosemary chicken breasts, tabouli, and several other scrumptious salads plus chocolate brownies for dessert. After dinner, Blake smokes a cigar and I consume the rest of the champagne. While my cell phone may not get Wi-Fi here, I can still use it to look at the many photos of our beautiful children. But Blake won't let me, knowing how emotional I'll get.

By the time he's done with his cigar, the sun, a big red ball of fire, is almost set. The pink-streaked sky is darkening and hints at a full moon. Under different circumstances, I'd admire the breathtaking sunset more. The temperature dropping, I put my sweatshirt back on and then clean up. There's nothing left over. Wanting to preserve our limited supply of bottled water, I head to the ocean to rinse off our plates and utensils. The gentle ebb and flow of the ocean is like soft music and tickles my toes.

When I return to our campsite, the bra-fire still blazing, Blake is on his knees in the sand building something.

Blake may not be handy at home, but one of the things he excels at is building sandcastles. He's built countless ones with our kids, who have both inherited his talent.

"Blake, are you building a sandcastle?" I ask as I store the plates and utensils in the brown paper bag.

"Not exactly."

I study his elaborate creation. It's about three feet

tall with rows of finger holes for windows. My eyes stay on him as he takes one of the sticks I collected and starts to etch something in the sand.

"Tah-dah!" he blurts proudly.

I read what he's written. "Welcome to the Ritz Carlton." I can't help laughing.

"Yup, baby. Nothing but the finest. Welcome to our luxury 5-Star accommodations." He sweeps his arm out, bringing my attention to the life raft. "King-size bed and *special* amenities included." Then, he gropes *his* special amenity. "We're *glamping* it."

"Glamping?" I can't stop laughing.

"It's the way rich people camp. Glamour camping." He tells me how his parents used to take him and his sister Marcy on *glamping* trips when they were youngsters. To deluxe, oversized cabins and tents, complete with gourmet food and every creature comfort possible, from the shores of Santa Barbara to the jungles of Africa.

"We'll have to do that with the kids sometime when we get back."

If we get back. My laughter dies down and I get serious.

"Blake, is this where we're going to sleep?"

"Yup. The plane feels like a sauna, and those seats won't be comfortable." He gazes up at the sky. "And you can't beat this view."

I gaze up too. The night is beautiful. The navy-blue

sky lit up by the full moon and a flurry of stars. The ocean is calm. The air balmy.

"I'm beat," says Blake with a yawn.

Suddenly, the intensity of the day and the effect of the champagne get to me. Blake and I agree to call it a night. We retreat inside our sleeping quarters.

Naked, blanketed by the warmth of his loving body spooned around mine, I close my eyes. It's actually more comfortable than I imagined. Delicious and sensual. Outside, I hear the soft sounds of the ocean's waves ebbing and flowing. Optimism flows through me. Hoping that if I wake up tomorrow, I will have survived today. And find myself one day closer to being reunited with my family.

When I wake up in the morning after a delicious night's sleep, Blake's gone!

Chapter 6

Blake

DAY 2

Close to our spot on the beach, I see Jen running toward me. She's wearing the dress she wore last night. My bare feet dig into the sand as I jog her way. Almost colliding, I take her into my arms. She pulls away.

"Jesus, Blake, where have you been?" Her voice is a mix of tearful, angry, and relieved.

I draw her back into me. "I got up early and went for a run. Halfway around the island. It was exhilarating." *And it got rid of my boner.*

"Why didn't you tell me?" Anger dominates her voice.

"You were sleeping. And looked so peaceful." *And so frickin' hot, I wanted to fuck you.*

She lets out an exhale, breathing out her anger. "Don't ever do that again. It totally freaked me out."

"I'm sorry. Here. A peace offering . . . Breakfast." I

dig into a pocket and hold out a granola bar I snagged off the plane. She grabs it, unpeels the wrapping, and takes a bite.

She chews it and after swallowing, I crush my mouth on hers. Her lips resist mine, feel hesitant. It's not the passionate, submissive kiss I'm used to. Is she still mad at me?

"What's wrong, tiger?"

"Blake, why haven't any rescue planes circled the island? Your father would have contacted the hotel by now. And the authorities."

She's right. A shudder runs through me. What the fuck is going on? I fumble for an excuse.

"The search and rescue team is probably on their way. You know, it can take twenty hours from the States to get here."

"But not if they were flying from Malé."

Malé is the capital of the Maldives, where the Gulf-stream was supposed to have landed, but couldn't on account of the strong winds. She's right as always—it's only a couple hours away. Unsettling thoughts fill my head. Maybe my father never contacted the hotel. Or they didn't see us at night. Or there's some other problem. My muscles tense at the possibilities.

"What should we do, Blake?"

When it comes to getting out of here, I don't have an answer. I hesitate before responding.

"Babe, let's explore this island while the weather's

still cool." The early morning ocean breeze sweeps across my cheeks. It invigorates me.

"And let's not worry."

My acting skills have served me well over the years. I'm the world's best pitchman. Selling one TV series after another to broadcasters around the world. Today, to my wife, I'm pitching something different. Unscripted. Intangible. Maybe inaccessible.

Hope . . . hoping my tiger will buy into my words. The naked truth: in my heart of hearts, I'm as worried as she is. But I don't let my brave tiger know that. I take her hand and we start to stroll.

"Maybe we'll find a Starbucks."

After performing all our morning rituals the Mother Nature way, including a quick cleansing bath in the ocean where we brushed our teeth, we prepare for our outing. Jen's wearing another calf-length sundress but has put a blouse over it so she doesn't burn. Her skin is fair unlike mine, which tans easily. She's nonetheless sprayed a ton of sunscreen all over my bare torso. We're both wearing hats—her a floppy straw one, me a Dodgers' baseball cap—and sunglasses. Slung over our shoulders are our backpacks and she's additionally carrying her tote. Sturdy sneakers complete our ensembles.

"We look like tourists," Jen laughs.

"Maybe we'll run into some others."

"Wishful thinking."

"Maybe if we find the local mall."

"That would be good. You owe me some new bras."

"I have my credit card."

"We're definitely going to need it," she deadpans back.

Twenty minutes later, we're exploring a new part of the island. It's a tropical rainforest, filled with exotic palm trees, fruit trees, and other vegetation, including unusual wild flowers.

"Wow! This is amazing!" Jen's eyes grow wide, as they roam our jungle-like surroundings. "I feel like I'm in a Gauguin painting."

"Yeah, it's definitely cool."

"Do you think there are wild animals hiding around?"

With a loud growl, I leap in front of her and make lion hands at her and bear my teeth. "GRRRRRR!"

She screams. "Jesus, Blake, that scared me. Stop freaking me out."

"C'mon, tiger. Show your teeth."

With a ferocious snarl, she narrows her eyes at me, and then clawing her hands, she jumps me, her feet leaving the ground. Holding her up, I can't miss an opportunity to kiss her. Smacking my lips onto hers, I give her a hard, hot kiss as she digs her fingernails into my back.

"That's better, my wild beast," she purrs after I break the kiss and set her down.

Grinning, I take her hand again. "Let's do some more exploring."

"Good idea, Robinson Crusoe."

We continue to walk through the rainforest, marveling at the foliage and the colorful butterflies flitting around. We even see some parrots hanging out in a palm tree. The din of other buzzing insects and chirping birds fills the air, creating a melodic tropical symphony. Along the way, Jen gathers some wild flowers, which she wants to put into her hair and use to adorn tonight's dinner. We also collect some exotic fruits—papayas, mangoes, plantains, as well as something that resembles a prickly avocado. Jen's tote is now heavy, so we each take a handle.

The temperature rises as we get deeper into the forest. In the heat and humidity, I feel my skin getting sticky from the mixture of sweat and sunscreen. Plus, it's getting really buggy. I swat at a mosquito. I've had enough of this place.

"C'mon, baby. Let's head back."

With the weighty bag and the humidity, my tiger doesn't need any convincing. With her blouse clinging to her, we head back to the beach.

Along the way, I collect some twigs and pieces of bark that will be good for our fire later as well as several long thick sticks that might be good for something else. Maybe I'll construct a fence around our deluxe accommodations. I smile to myself. Just call me Blake the Builder. Move over, Bob!

Halfway back, Calamity Jen almost trips. I grab her just in time. She casts her eyes down and gets her wish. The one thing not in our bag.

"Cool beans! A coconut!" Though we saw many along the way hanging from the tall palms, they were too high up to reach. Even with the long sticks we found. I bend down and toss it into the tote, surprised by how heavy it is.

"Blake, do you think you can open it? I really want to try coconut milk."

"Sure. Remember, I was a Boy Scout."

"Yeah, right."

After a quick dip in the ocean to cool off, Jen and I prepare lunch. A fruit salad using all the delicacies we found in the forest. Using one of our plastic knives, Jen slices up the fruit while I work on the coconut. Let me rephrase that, the fucking coconut. My Swiss Army knife is just not cutting it. No pun intended. I need a cleaver or a sledgehammer.

"How are you doing?" Glancing my way, my wife flashes me a wry smile.

"Fine." I stab the word at her.

"Oh, so you were a Boy Scout." Her voice is dripping with sarcasm.

"I sliced open frogs in Boy Scout camp."

"Hmm . . . Boy Scout camp. That's a new one."

"Pay attention to cutting up the mango. I can't afford to have you slice open your finger. There's no emergency room here."

I've been to the ER with Jen more times than I care to count. The first time, before we got married, to urgent care when she stepped on a shard of glass after breaking up with me . . . second at the altar when she began to hemorrhage right through her dress . . . then there was the bagel cutting incident after our honeymoon when she almost lost her finger . . . the rollerblading wipeout at Venice Beach after which she had to get her knee stitched up . . . oh yeah, can't forget the time she spilled piping hot coffee on her hand . . . or the little spill when we went skiing in Sun Valley that landed her back on crutches . . . and that's just in the first two years of our marriage. She didn't earn the nickname Calamity Jen for a lack of orgasms.

"Don't worry, Blake. I'm doing just fine." She finishes slicing the mango and moves on to one of the bananas.

My muscles tense. The frickin' coconut is driving me crazy. The next time I stab it with my knife I plunge it so deep I can't get the damn blade out of the shell without breaking the knife.

"Balls!" I yell in frustration.

"What's the matter, my love?" There's so much mockery in Jen's singsong voice that I feel my blood heat.

"Nothing!"

"I'm so looking forward to trying coconut milk. And maybe I'll put some of the coconut meat into the fruit salad."

Frustration is plowing through me like a freight train. It gives way to rage. Simmering mad, I feel like I'm going to implode. I'm Superman, but I can't defeat my new worst enemy. The coconut monster. Maybe if I had a hard surface, I could just chuck the damn thing against it and it would split open. My eyes roam . . . and badda bing! I have an idea.

Holding the coconut face down with the knife stuck in it, I spring to my feet and take angry, giant steps toward the plane.

"Where are you going, Blake?" calls out Jen.

My face scrunched with fierce determination, I don't answer her. I continue my march until I'm about twenty feet away from the plane. Calling on all my strength and my best Little League pitching skills, I hurl the coconut at the aircraft. A curve ball. My eyes stay on it as it travels at lightning speed. It hits the body of the plane with a raucous bang. YES! Score one for me. Upon impact, the coconut splits open and my knife falls to the sand. With a jog, I go collect my booty, putting the knife back into my pocket, and sprint back to Jennifer.

"Hey, look!" With a shit-eating grin, I hold out the coconut halves in the palms of my hands.

Jennifer's eyes bug out of their sockets; her jaw drops to her chest. She gasps. "Oh my God!"

This is not an awestruck "oh my God." It's laced with horror.

"What's wrong?" I ask anxiously as she clasps a hand to her gaping mouth.

"Your chest!"

I cast my eyes down. They grow as wide as hers.

Jesus Christ!

I'm the one who needs to go to an emergency room!

Chapter 7

Blake

"Don't move," orders Jennifer as she squirts a dollop of white cream onto my skin.

I glance down. I'm horrified. Dozens of red welts dot my chest from my pecs all the way down to my hips. There are also some scattered along my arms and legs.

"Mosquito bites," says Jen matter-of-factly.

Mosquito bites? Everyone knows mosquitos can be deadly.

Malaria!

Dengue Fever!

West Nile Virus!

Zika!

Panic grips me like a manacle. I'm going to die!

"Jen, what are we going to do? I need to be airlifted to a hospital!"

"Blake, calm down. They're just mosquito bites." She dabs some more cream on the welts.

"What are you doing?"

"I'm just putting on some cortisone cream to get the swelling down and to take away the redness."

"But people can die from mosquito bites!"

"Blake, you're such a hypochondriac."

It's true. While I could take a knife to my heart for her, I'm really bad when it comes to getting sick. Jen always likes to rub it in that with the slightest sniffle I'm on death's bed. Quick! Call the ambulance!

"How do you know for sure I won't die?" I ask skeptically.

"I just do." Another dab. "You're *That Man,* remember?"

Her invincible superhero. I'm beginning to question myself.

"How come you didn't get bit?"

"First of all, I was wearing long sleeves and a calf-length dress. And secondly, the only mosquitos who bite are female and they prefer juicy men." She surveys my bitten-up body. "Those mosquitos must have had the hots for you."

For the first time in my life, I wish I wasn't hot as sin. God's gift to mosquitos.

She finishes applying the ointment on the welts. Then, she takes out a bottle with a pink liquid inside it from her first-aid kit. Along with a couple of Q-tips.

"What's that?" I ask as she soaks the cotton heads with the pink stuff.

"Calamine lotion."

"Will it hurt?"

"Not at all. The calamine will help with the itching and healing process."

I watch as she dots the welts with a pink-coated Q-tip, having to dip it into the bottle several times and use more than one.

"Okay, all done." She bursts into laughter.

"What's so funny?"

"You, Mr. Pink Polka Dot Man."

I glance down at myself. I'm a sight for sore eyes. I look like I belong in some kind of freak show.

"How long will it take for them to go away?" I ask as she puts away the cortisone cream and the calamine.

"A couple of days. The salt water will be good for them. The most important thing is that you don't scratch them and get an infection."

Again, my mind jumps to the worst possible scenario. My body covered with head to toe festering boils. The pus dripping down my torso and my limbs. My infected skin feverish. My breathing labored.

Jennifer cuts into my lethal thoughts. "I'm going to make you take some Benadryl tonight. It's an antihistamine that will also help get down the swelling and stop the itching."

"Why can't I have some now?"

"It'll make you drowsy."

Drowsy is the last thing I want to be on this mosquito-infested island. I need to be alert so I can swat the little fuckers—squish them with my hands—if they dare to come near me again. Suddenly, my dick feels itchy. Oh no! I didn't check. Maybe I got bitten there too.

I scratch my crotch. "Jen, I have a bad feeling about something." Poor Mr. Burns!

"What, Blake?"

"My equipment . . . I think they got me there."

"Pull down your shorts. Let's take a look-see."

I drop my trunks and she gets to her knees. Squinting, she carefully studies my cock and then wraps her hands around it to examine the underside. Holy Moses. She's giving me a boner.

"I don't see anything."

"My balls are itching."

She fondles my balls. Holy shit. I'm about to jump out of my skin.

"Um, uh, Nurse Jen, I'm sure I got bitten. Look, my cock is swelling up. And it feels really hot and tingly."

"Really?" Her voice grows seductively lower.

"Really. I think my cock needs emergency attention."

She circles her slender fingers around the base again, applying a little pressure. "Yes, Mr. Burns, I think your cock needs special treatment."

On my next heated breath, she trails warm, wet, soft kisses down my shaft. I jolt at the sensation, forcing my eyes not to close. When she returns to the crown after another line of kisses along my length, she glances up at me.

"Is this making you feel better, Mr. Burns?"

"More," I mutter, my breath stuttering.

With a smug smile, she focuses her attention on my crown, running her lips over the surface, licking and flicking it with her tongue. My dick stiffening, she opens her mouth wide and completely wraps her lips around the head until it disappears. Still squeezing the base, she sucks it hard and then glides her mouth down my thick rigid length, dragging her tongue along the underside. My back arching, I hiss as she makes her way back up. My body's sizzling with electricity. My nerve endings buzzing, my skin ablaze.

"Jesus, baby."

Moving her other hand to my balls, she continues her ministrations, taking me all the way. I can still feel my cock expanding against the hollows of her cheeks as she starts massaging my nuts. I moan and groan with the insane pleasure she's giving me, now only able to silently beg for her not to stop. My prescient tiger reads my mind. Her firm hand pumps my base as her gifted mouth glides up and down, both picking up speed in concert. I plant my palms on her shoulders to keep my balance. After ten years of marriage, my tiger still knows how to give a man head. Not just any head. Fucking mind-blowing head. The kind that fries your brain and makes everything a haze. An out-of-body experience. A euphoric sensation crackles down my spine and climbs up thighs. My whole body stiffens and my balls contract—the telltale signs as my cock begins to spasm.

"Baby, get ready. I'm going to come in your mouth."

With another squeeze of the base, her wet, luscious mouth skates one more time down my thick, pulsing length and—*Boom!*—with a raw, feral grunt, my seed shoots down her throat. As she makes her way back up, I slowly pull out of her mouth, my cock glistening and spent. My eyes half-mast, I watch her swallow with satisfaction. She licks her upper lip, her oh so talented tongue languorously making a semi-circle across it. It's such a total turn-on when she does that.

"Baby, that was fucking amazing." Mr. Burns is one happy camper. Or should I say *glamper?*

She gazes up at me with those twinkling green ti-gress eyes. "So, Blake, how do your mosquito bites feel?"

I trace her shimmering lips with my index finger as blissful numbness takes hold of me.

"What bites?"

Chapter 8

Jennifer

In one's imagination, being with the man you love on a deserted island sounds divine. Idyllic. Dreamy. In reality, it's not. In addition to the hardships we've encountered, it can also get boring. There's only so much swimming, hiking, and screwing you can do—though the latter counts for a lot. Thank goodness, we brought all our electronic devices. While we don't have Wi-Fi, my Kindle is loaded up with some romance books and psychological suspense thrillers, and my iPod is filled with my favorite songs. Blake has also brought along his phone and iPod as well as his laptop though he promised not to do any work on our second honeymoon. In the hours that pass, we take a break from the sun and hang out in the shaded life raft. Blake reviews some contracts on his laptop while I read a new book by Nelle L'Amour: *Remember Me.* While I love working in children's programming, I sometimes miss programming My Sin-TV, the women's erotica network I started that catapulted my entertainment career.

We also brought along a Scrabble game and a deck of cards. We decide to play Scrabble, me, as usual beating Blake's sorry ass. Then, we play tic-tac-toe, with Blake drawing the squares in the sand with a twig he found and using the things we've collected so far. Blake's banana leaves beat my seashells three times out of four. We laugh about playing strip poker, but in our almost naked states, there's virtually nothing to take off.

The day goes by quickly and soon it's time for dinner. We're both ravenous again. Blake heads back to the plane to see if he can scrounge up more food. While he's in the plane, I set up the blanket with plates, glasses, and utensils. I put some of the exotic flowers we gathered into one of our empty plastic bottles in the center, using the tiniest bit of water. Our table, so to speak, looks lovely. My mother would be proud of me. As I add a yellow bloom to the array, my eyes catch sight of Blake deplaning, carrying only a bottle in his hand. As swoon-worthy as he is even with all his bites, he looks glum. Defeated. He trudges toward me.

"Bad news, baby."

My eyebrows lift. Dread fills my empty stomach. "What's the matter?"

"I found one more bag of food, but it spoiled because of the heat. The only thing that was worth taking was this bottle of wine. And it's warm." He holds it up. A California chardonnay. *Naked Grape.* One of our favorites.

"So, we'll drink our dinner."

Blake is not amused by my little joke. "I should have left the engine on so the plane stayed air-conditioned. Plus, maybe if the landing lights of the aircraft had been on last night, a rescue team would have seen us."

He looks and sounds so dejected. This is the first time since we left LA he's sunk into a deep funk. The vulnerable expression on his face is one I've seen before. When he sat with me right after my surgery, waiting for my prognosis. Was my tumor malignant or not?

My poor baby! He takes so much onto himself to protect our family and me. He thinks he's a superhero and forgets he's only human. There are times I have to be strong for him and mentally don my Wonder Woman costume. This is one of them. His head bowed, I lovingly wrap my arms around him, pressing my forehead against his.

"Blake, baby, stop beating yourself up. Things are what they are. This situation isn't easy. It's hard to think straight all the time."

"I fucked up."

"No, you didn't. We can have fruit for dinner. There's still some left."

"Baby, if I have more fruit, I'm going to pollute the ocean."

Truthfully, me too.

Holding each other, we let a stretch of silence embrace us. Only the sound of the gentle waves lulls in our ears. Then suddenly, he lifts his head and flicks my nose. The glum expression on his face has brightened. His eyes are lit with excitement. My suspicion is that one of his light bulb ideas has come to him. This could be good. Or it could be bad. Very bad. I hold my breath in anticipation as he shares it.

"Babe, I have a great idea. Let's go fishing."

What? Fishing? My I'd-rather-be-on-a-yacht husband and shopping at Saks Fifth Avenue went to a sporting goods store and brought along a fishing rod? I ask him point blank.

"No, but I know how to make one."

YUP. Can you hear me mentally punch the "p"? He doesn't even have to say it. Boy Scout camp.

On my next breath: Fishing. Rod. In. Progress.

Blake has retrieved one of the long sticks he found earlier in the rainforest.

"Babe, do you by chance have any dental floss?"

Of course, I do. I'm a flossing fanatic. I scurry to my duffel and find the dispenser of premium-waxed floss. Hurrying back, I hand it to Blake.

He smiles. "Perfect."

I watch as he pulls out the glossy cord and wraps it around the lower third of the long wood stick, letting several feet dangle. At least ten.

"We need a small weight," he says.

I mentally search my suitcases, trying to determine if I have one.

Nada.

"What about my wedding band?"

"Jesus, Jen, are you insane? That's supposed to last for an eternity."

I bow my head in shame, staring at the platinum band that accompanies my exquisite snowflake diamond engagement ring. The band that matches Blake's and unites our hearts and our souls. The sparkling diamonds of the cluster ring blur as I grow teary-eyed. My heart weeps. I feel terrible. What made me offer it up?

"Blake, I'm sorry." My voice small, I fidget with the rings. "I don't know what made me say that."

Blake tenderly tilts up chin and I meet his forgiving eyes. "It's okay, baby. This place looks like paradise, but it ain't. We're under a lot of stress. Just promise me that you won't say or do any crazy things again."

I nod. "I promise, my love. I won't."

Blake flashes a grateful smile and pecks a kiss on my forehead. "Good, now put your thinking cap back on. What can we use as a weight?"

I search my mind again, and suddenly, my spirits brighten. I have a cheap locket with me that I was going to have a Maldives artisan copy in gold. I hurry back to my suitcase, search for it, and then return to Blake. I hold it in my palm.

"Will this work?"

He takes it from me. "What is this piece of junk?"

"Some cheap old locket I found at the flea market."

He twitches a smile. "It's perfect."

I watch as he loops the floss through the bezel over and over and then knots it. Confession: I'm beginning to think he may have been a Boy Scout.

A six-inch strand of floss hangs from the locket.

"We need a few more things."

"Like what?"

"Like a hook."

I think again. I have a few pairs of cheap chandelier earrings. Impulse purchases from Zara online. I mention them to him.

His brows knit as his lips twist. "The hooks will probably be way too flimsy to hold a fish. Think again."

My mind goes back into think-mode. And idea comes to me quickly.

"Blake, do you, by chance, have anything packed that came straight from the drycleaner?" My husband loves to send his wardrobe to the drycleaner, especially on business trips, so they'll come back on wire hangers and wrapped in plastic. It makes for wrinkle-free packing in his hanging bag.

"Yeah, one suit."

"Maybe you can figure out a way to break off the hooked part of the hanger."

Blake's eyes light up. "That's a great idea! I can use my Swiss Army knife." He draws me in for a quick, appreciative smack on the lips. "Baby, have I recently told you how much I love you because you're so smart?"

I grin sheepishly. "Yes, but you can tell me again and again."

Over the next five minutes, I watch as my husband uses one of the serrated blades of his Swiss Army knife to detach the wiry hanger hook. He bends it a little and then expertly attaches it to the end of the floss. He smiles proudly at his handiwork. I must admit it's impressive.

"Baby, we need one more thing . . . bait."

"What about a piece of fruit?"

Blake's response: "I. Don't. Think. So." He scrunches his forehead in deep thought. "Do you have any of those gummy worms you love?"

I cock a brow. "Yes, why?"

"They make good fish bait. We used them one summer at camp."

"But that was probably freshwater lake fishing. This is salt-water ocean fishing. There's a difference."

"Hey, everyone loves candy. It's worth a shot."

Fifteen minutes later, I'm standing waist-deep in the water with Blake, his body blanketing me from behind. We hold the pole together, his large hands covering mine.

A half-hour later, we move our position, to the right and a little deeper. Still no takers.

"Blake, this is futile. I'm hungry. Let's go back and we'll dine on granola bars and wine."

"Patience, baby. I'm feeling it."

And then suddenly, I'm feeling it too. For real. A tug. A big tug.

"We've landed a big one!" Blake shouts excitedly. "Help me bring him in."

The fish is a fighter. He jumps in and out of the water as we take steps backward toward the shore. My wrists feel like they're going to snap off.

"Blake, we're going to lose him!"

The force of the fish is daunting. I'm worried our pole will break. Or he'll loosen himself from the hook.

"Hang on, baby. He's a keeper." Blake grunts as he battles the fish.

We keep stepping back until we're in shallow water. The fish flaps madly as Blake and I drag him along the floor of the ocean. For the first time, I get a close look at him. Silvery with flecks of green and blue, he's about two feet long with bulging eyes and a wide-open mouth full of sharp, spikey teeth. He looks mean. Desperate to free himself and bite us.

Blake drags him onto shore. As the gentle waves wash over him, the fish continues to flap madly, doing somersaults in the air.

"Tiger, step aside," orders Blake, his face intense as

he wrestles with our catch.

Wasting no time, I jump away, distancing myself from Blake and the fish. Suddenly, an unexpected wave of sadness sweeps over me. Despite how angry and menacing he looks, I feel sorry for the doomed creature. Maybe it's a reflection of my own pending sense of doom.

"Blake, how are we going to get him off the hook?" My voice is tearful. I feel like I'm going to burst out crying. I don't know why I feel this way when I've eaten fish countless times. In fact, when I go out to chic restaurants with Blake, I almost always order fish, be it a salmon filet, swordfish steak, or ahi-tuna. And I love tuna fish sandwiches and sushi too. I've just never eaten a whole bone-in fish—fresh from the ocean– with its head, fins, and tail intact. Or seen one take its last breath. Maybe on this island, I sympathize with him. Life's short. Endangered. Finite.

Blake answers my question as the struggling fish starts to lose steam. "Unless you want me to lose my fingers, we're just going to let him run his course."

"Oh God, Blake! I can't handle this!"

The fish's breathing slows and he stops writhing. Why am I watching?

Blake sets our makeshift fishing pole on the wet sand. Stepping back, he puts an arm around me. "Baby, you remember our New Year's tradition?"

I nod. Every New Years Eve we cook live lobsters

and name them after a person we loathe as we put them into the pot of boiling water.

"Good. You have the honors to name this fish after the person you despise the most. Just don't go all political on me."

Feeling a little better, I search my mind. Only one name surfaces. The skanky bitch who almost cost Blake his life. And almost ended that of his best friend— Brandon Taylor, the star of the long-running Conquest Broadcasting series, *Kurt Kussler*. After some jail time, the delusional witch got out, published a bestselling book—*I Put the It in Bitch*—and got her own reality series on another network. I spit out her name.

"Katrina."

A half-hour later, we're devouring her. Washing her down with our chardonnay. Maybe next year at this time, if there is a next year, she'll fall down again. Hard.

Chapter 9

Blake

G etting over her initial squeamishness, I must say I was very impressed with my tiger's survivalist skills. She even helped scale the fish using my Swiss Army knife. But adorably, she looked away as I fileted it and washed away the blood with some seawater. We both decided to leave the head on because it would be way more fun to eat Katrina with her eyes on us. Jen doused the fish with a bit of the white wine and some fresh mango juice and then we grilled it in the fire I made, wrapping it in the foiled containers we still had from last night's Whole Foods dinner. It tasted totally delicious and went great with the wine.

Buzzed from the wine and smoking a cigar while I listen to some music on my iPod, I watch as my beautiful wife cleans up and gets our "deluxe" bed ready for the night, sweeping out the sand. She's wearing another one of her floral sundresses, this one only coming to her thighs. I wonder if she's wearing little lace panties. If she is, she won't be for long.

After all these years, I still find my wife sexy as hell. There's no other woman I could have married. My old man was right. When he hired her, he told me she'd be good for me. On second thought, actually he was wrong. She's perfect for me. In every way.

Besides being beautiful to look at, she's brilliant, thoughtful, and down-to-earth. The only person on Earth who can keep me grounded, she turned a self-centered playboy into a caring man. Taught me what it was to love, cherish, and protect another. Helped me build Conquest Broadcasting into the biggest and most successful broadcasting network in the world. Helped me reconcile my differences with my older sister. And best of all, gave me the two most incredible children in the world. Leo and his sister Maeve, both whom I adore more than life itself.

She's the best wife, lover, and soul mate a man could ever have. And I couldn't ask for a better mother for my kids. I often think back to how we met. It was a freak thing. She was celebrating her engagement to her dweeby dentist boyfriend at an LA hotspot and played a game of Truth or Dare with her friends. Her dare: to kiss me blindfolded. That kiss was the best damn kiss I ever had. Just thinking about it gives me testicular tingles. But then things got a little crazy with my vengeful, twin-powered hook-ups and I lost her in the crowd. Then, what do you know, she showed up in my office the next day to start her new job. Though she was wearing glasses, I recognized her immediately and something about her greenest of green eyes drove me crazy. Then, in our interview, she had to pretend to have an orgasm (HA!—all part of the job!) and my cock went into a frenzy. It was right then and there that I decided this girl was a tiger. Man, could she roar. I had to have her.

That's when things got a little tricky. She was engaged, but I didn't let that stop me. Enter Operation Dickwick. My mission: To eliminate the competition. And I did by catching her prick-of-a-boyfriend cheating on her with his dental hygienist on my phone. When I cleverly emailed her the footage (which would later bite me in the ass and almost end our relationship) that was it for Dickwick. *Sayonara.* My turn to move in and that opportunity came up during a business trip to Vegas. We got a little buzzed and when the lounge singer sang, "The First Time Ever I Saw Your Face," that was it for me. When I took her into my arms and danced with her, I knew it was more than lust. I was totally fucking in love with the feisty, green-eyed, chestnut-haired beauty from Idaho.

"Blake—" My tiger's voice cuts into my memories.

"Yeah, baby?" I take out my earbuds.

"Do you want to take a walk?"

My gaze shifts in her direction. She looks ravishing. Her toned limbs luminescent in the moonlight, her dress gently blowing in the ocean breeze along with her up swept hair. I stare at her exquisite face, aglow in the campfire, her green eyes glittering like two stars that have fallen from the sky.

The first time ever I saw her face . . . Yes, I thought the sun rose in her eyes. And even before that I felt the earth move in my hand, the first time I ever kissed her mouth.

The song plays in my head. A sensation that I can't put into words falls over me. It's like a fire that's burning from the inside out, consuming every atom of my being. A love so deep it hurts. I respond to her question.

"Baby, go get your iPod."

Without questioning me, she pivots and heads toward her backpack. While she's riffling for the device, I put out my cigar in the sand and search my library of songs. It doesn't take me long to find it.

She returns to me quickly and sits down facing me.

"You want to just hang out and listen to music?"

"Give me your iPod."

Again, without questions, she hands it over. I quickly program it. I wrap the band around her upper arm and then fasten mine around my bicep. I help her to her feet and draw her close to me.

"Dance with me, tiger," I breathe against her neck, before putting the buds into our ears.

With love in her eyes, she gazes up at me. A faint smile, that's more wistful than lustful, fixes on her kissable lips, as our song plays in her ears.

No more words.

I wrap my arms around her, clutching her gorgeous ass, while she loops hers around my neck and rests her head on my chest. Our bodies glued together. Heat to heat. Organ to organ. Heartbeat to heartbeat.

Every sound and worry in the world blocked out, we slow dance to the song that changed our lives forever. The song we played at our third and final wedding. The one that sealed our love forever. Taking one small step at a time as we sway, our feet sink into the soft, warm sand.

Under the moon.

Under the stars.

The heavens.

Oneness.

Us.

If there's such a thing as Paradise, this is it.

Chapter 10
Blake

For the second day in a row, I wake up super early. I glance down at my watch. It's not even six o'clock. Turning, I stare at the angel still sound asleep next to me. I brush a few stray hairs off her forehead and give her a light kiss on her lips. Those lips that were all over me last night in one of the most passionate and sensual nights I've ever had. A night of intense lovemaking. Of cherishing the one you're with, knowing that tomorrow isn't promised to anyone. Especially us. One arm draped over me, the other outstretched above her, she stirs, and a small smile curls on the corners of her lips. I hope she's dreaming of me. Of us. Our future. And hope.

Careful not to wake her, I sit up, my head almost touching the top of our sleeping quarters, and cover my tiger with the blanket. Thanks to a mosquito resistant wristband Jen fastened on me, I haven't gotten any more nasty bug bites. And thanks to the cortisone cream which she reapplied and the Benadryl, most of the existing bites have gone down and aren't too itchy. The pink calamine lotion has peeled off on account of the humidity, so I'm no longer Mr. Pink Polka Dot Man. And thank fuck, I feel fine with no sign of an infection or a disease.

My gaze fixes on the horizon. Unlike yesterday, the sun's nowhere in sight. Instead, the sky is overcast, the sea a shade of grayish blue. It's choppy. Rougher than usual, with visible, audible waves crashing against the shoreline. The humidity is thick and it's windy.

The weather conditions concern me. But maybe this is typical at this time of the year. And the grayness will lift. Angsting a bit and not wanting to wake up my tiger, I leave her a note so she won't worry. I let her know that I've gone for a run around the island and that I'll be back soon. I place it under her outstretched hand. Then, I crawl out of the tent, slipping on some board shorts, a T-shirt, my baseball cap along with my Ray-Bans. Before I set off, I grab my iPod and rearrange the seashells surrounding our campfire site into a heart. A little poem dances in my head.

> My tiger is my fire.
> My inner light.
> All that I desire.
> The love of my life.

While I'm no Maya Angelou, I've come a long way from writing silly limericks. I think about etching the words in the sand, but with the wind blowing, it's unlikely they'll last for more than a few minutes.

Heading toward the shore, I start off slowly and then pick up my pace until I'm running a steady seven-minute mile in my bare feet. The run keeps my mind off all the things I don't want to think about. Mostly, the disturbing question of why a search and rescue team hasn't shown up yet; it's beginning to freak me out. Getting into the zone, I let it go and just focus on my breathing. Ten minutes in, I break into a sweat and continue for another few miles until I can no longer bear my wet, clingy T-shirt. Stopping for a minute, I pull it over my head and decide to chuck it. I have a whole suitcase of T-shirts with me.

Catching my breath, I'm suddenly aware of the weather changes. The air drips with humidity, and storm clouds move like stealth bombers across the menacing sky. I look out to sea and study the fierce waves. Tall, ferocious gray beasts whose jagged white crests snap at me like fangs. A strong wind blows against my bare chest, at the same time kicking up sand in my direction. In the distance, I see palm trees swaying, their giant fronds flapping against the sky. Electricity fills the air.

My muscles tensing, I don't like what I'm seeing, hearing, or feeling. Not one fucking bit. A major storm is coming in. Panic hits me like a bolt of lightning. I've got to get back to our campsite.

To my tiger!

Not wasting a second, I turn around and run back as fast as I can. Sprinting. My limbs, my lungs burning. The fire inside me propelled by fear.

Chapter 11

Jennifer

The sound of crashing waves awakens me. Despite being stranded on this island, last night was one of the most incredible nights of my life. Dancing in Blake's arms to our song, then making beautiful love all night long until I fell asleep in his arms like a baby. The fear of not being rescued didn't enter my mind once.

My eyes still closed, I stretch my arm across the blanket. My heart jumps. Blake's not there! Alarm spreading across my skin, I snap my eyes open and thankfully find a note, letting me know he's gone for a run. I breathe a sigh of relief and climb out of the tent. Almost instantly, my lips slide into an ear-to-ear smile at the sight of the heart of seashells surrounding our campfire. Oh, how I love *that* man!

I do my morning business, brush my teeth and then my hair. My hair feels like a rat's nest, matted from the salty sea, sweat, and the humidity. My soft waves have become knotted, sticky curls. And my scalp's full of sand. When Blake comes back, I'm going to treat

myself to a shampoo and rinse it with a lot of conditioner. It's been three days or is it four? I'm losing track
of time. All that matters is that we get through today.
And pray we'll be rescued.

Donning a pair of shorts and a tank top, I grab a
granola bar and a papaya for breakfast. I notice we're
almost out of fruit. There's just a couple of small
bananas left, leaving us with very little to eat for lunch.
The weather, unlike the past few days, is gloomy and
cooler. There's a strong ocean breeze and the sea is
grayer. Taking the last bite of my tasty papaya, I decide
to venture back into the rainforest to gather more fruit.
And this time, I want to take photos. I grab my
Conquest sweatshirt, tying it around my waist, put on
my sneakers, and then spray on some sunscreen and
bug repellent. I leave Blake a note under one of the
shells. With my backpack slung over my shoulders, my
phone inside it, I take off.

A half hour into my trek, I start to get antsy. Unlike
yesterday when the warm sun lit the way, its rays
peeking through the palm fronds, today the dense
rainforest is dark and dreary. The butterflies that we
saw flitting around yesterday seem to be hiding. The
hum of buzzing bugs mingles with a strange clicking
sound, creating an unsettling percussional symphony.

The temperature dropping, I take off my backpack and put on my sweatshirt. Slinging my heavy, almost filled up bag back on my shoulders, I decide to head back. The wind picks up and the palm trees sway. The sky above me darkens as a sudden clap of thunder startles me. My heart hammers. On my next anxious breath, I break into a jog.

The wind grows stronger; everything's blowing. Another clap of thunder. And then a bolt of lightning.

My heart racing, my breathing heavy, I suddenly realize I have no clue where I'm going. Or where I am. If only I'd made a trail like Hansel and Gretel. The air grows thicker, the forest almost black, as thunder rumbles again. Every tree, every shrub, every plant shakes. The sky is closing in. Terror fills every cell of my body. I'm lost in the forest on the verge of a storm

Chapter 12

Blake

Breathless, my thighs and calves on fire, I make it back to our campsite in less than thirty minutes. The sky has turned a menacing shade of gray, the angry ocean now darker than gunmetal. The wind is gusting at about forty miles an hour, and I'm thankful I'm wearing my Ray-Bans to shield my eyes from the maelstrom of sand.

I hurry to the life raft. Shit. It's empty. My eagle-sharp eyes circle the area. Jen is nowhere in sight. My blood pressure spikes as worry pulses through my bloodstream. Where the heck is she? Then, spinning around, I spot a piece of paper skittering down the beach. My heart racing, I chase after it. Bouncing from the sand to the air like a feather, it keeps blowing further and further away. Finally, I catch up with it. Stopping it from flying away with a stomp of my foot, I bend down and read it. My heart leaps to my throat. It's a note from Jen. Jesus Christ. She went back to the rainforest by herself. A clap of thunder bellows, followed by an electrifying flash of lightning. It's only a matter of time before all hell breaks loose. I sprint back to our campsite, hastily put on a sweatshirt and my running shoes, and then take off like the wind. Halfway there, my baseball cap flies off. There's no time to retrieve it. Every second I lose is one second I don't have to find my tiger. Battling the fierce wind, I pick up my pace.

By the time I get to the rainforest, it's pouring rain. I'm not talking a spring shower. This is a hurricane. A motherfucker monsoon. The wind is still gusting at some ungodly speed and once inside the pitch-dark forest, I can barely see two feet in front me. Yelling Jen's name, I tear through the dense foliage, narrowly dodging falling palm fronds, rockslides, and other fallen debris. Even giant trees are coming down.

"Jen! Jen!" I shout out at the top of my lungs—hoping my voice can be heard above the raging rain, gusting wind, and rustling palms. Not slowing down, I scream out her name over and over until my throat is raw and my voice is hoarse.

Fast and furious, my footsteps crunch in my ears. A frantic mixture of terror and desperation fills every morsel of my being. Panic sets in. Where the hell is she? Why isn't she answering?

Then suddenly, without warning, I feel myself tumbling. Fuck! I've tripped over a tree trunk! I try to break the fall, but I land flat on my face. Onto the soaked, muddy ground. The relentless pellets of rain still coming at me like bullets, the sky's like a sniper trying to take me down.

Move over, Katrina. Move over Fate. I've got a new bitch to deal with.

Fuck you, Mother Nature!

Chapter 13

Jennifer

I feel like I'm in a maze. A monstrous jungle I can't get out of.

Dizzy and fatigued, I will myself to keep moving. There's got to be a light at the end of this endless tunnel. Only one thought fills my head: Surviving.

The storm has worsened. Grown more intense. The torrential rain relentless, the gales ruthless. Thunder roars and lightning flashes, adding to the horror of my frightening reality: I may die. Breathing heavily, I forge ahead, tripping over rocks, fronds, and branches. Even a dead bat. My body is scratched up and my lungs are burning, but I need to ignore the pain.

Landing Blake's plane was terrifying enough, but this is far more terrifying. I can't close my eyes and hope for the best. I need to fight for my life. Fight for my beloved husband and my family. All that's dear to me.

A sudden gust of wind blasts through the forest. The palm trees sway madly, their giant fronds smacking each other like they're in a slapping match. My drenched ponytail whips across my face, stinging and blinding me. Maybe because I'm so tired, I feel like I'm going to be blown away. Battling the elements, I run to the nearest coconut tree and wrap my arms around it like it's my lover. The wind howls in my ears as the merciless rain assaults me. Pricking my flesh like a barrage of needles. My cheek pressed against the soaked bark, I start wailing. My shoulders heave as hot tears mingle with the rain, sobs wracking my body. My own personal tsunami.

I cling to the tree, lacing my fingers. Maybe staying in one place makes more sense. If I don't move, maybe Blake will find me. His tender, sexy voice fills my head as I flashback to that night—that unforgettable night he took down my assailant and saved my life.

"Baby, for you I'm invincible. I'm THAT man who's going to take care of you. Protect you from the monsters of the world. Slay them if I have to. And no one's going to stop me."

My superhero. All I can do is pray. Pray he's okay and on his way.

Another clap of thunder. Flash of lightning.

Then . . . BONK! The world fades to black.

Chapter 14

Blake

A frightened creature skitters over me. A lizard. I jolt. Coming to my senses, I pick myself up. While I'm covered in mud and debris, I'm not hurt except for a few scratches on my legs. The storm still raging, I tear through the rainforest in search of my wife. Shouting her name as loud as I can. I'm not giving up. Though my life is at stake, no fucking way. Hers comes first. Always has and always will. I made a vow on my wedding day to be there for her forever.

The rain continues to pound; the wind continues to gust. Soaked to the bone and panting like a dog, I narrowly escape a falling tree. My desperate search for my tiger borders on futile. I've been looking for close to an hour. Where the hell is she? Is she buried under the dense foliage, invisible to the naked eye? Pinned under a tree? Bitten by a snake? Attacked by some wild beast? Despair seizes me. I can't help but think the worst-case scenario: Is my wife still alive? Or is she dead?

On my next harsh breath, I banish the dark thought from my mind. My tiger is a survivor. A fighter! She's got to be alive! My throat burning, my lungs on fire, I call her name again.

"JENNNNNN!"

Then, suddenly, thrashing through the thicket, I see something. Not stopping, I swipe at the wet strands of hair that have fallen into my eyes and look closer. Christ. It's a limp body, sprawled beneath a palm tree. Wishing I could fly, I sprint up to it and fall to my knees. Breathless, I haul her into my arms.

My tiger! Unconscious. Her face drenched in blood. The rain rinsing it away to no avail. The river of red endless.

Cradling her, I notice a large coconut beside her. It must have fallen down and hit her head. Knocking her out. I hold up her ragdoll body. Her backpack's still on her. I can't tell if she's breathing. One shaky hand travels to her heart. I feel a beat. I see her gash.

"Tiger, can you hear me?"

No response.

"TIGER!" I yell louder.

"Talk to me, tiger!"

Nothing.

"Tiger!" I yell again.

FUCK. *Nada.*

On my next panicked breath, I sling her backpack over my shoulders and lift her into my arms. As thin as she is, she feels like a dead weight.

Battling the raging storm, I race out of the forest. Hoping I can get her to safety.

Not knowing what that means on this self-destructing island. Or what it means for us.

All I know is that my tiger is still alive. That *we* are still alive.

And that's all that matters.

Chapter 15

Blake

DAYS 4-6

The last three days have been a total nightmare. It hasn't stopped raining.

Don't ask me how I did it, but I managed to get my unconscious tiger to safety. The plane. Thanks to my legs being so strong from a combination of daily workouts and running up and down the Santa Monica stairs on weekends, I managed to run with her in my arms through the rainforest, then across the soaked beach, and in the nick of time, climb into the plane as a bolt of lightning came flying at us. Once inside the stuffy aircraft, I carried her to one of the side-by-side seats, got her out of her soaking wet clothes, and wrapped her in a spare blanket. I then laid her down across the seats, creating a makeshift bed. While it's hardly the luxurious bed of the Gulfstream with its gazillion dollar bedding, it's better than nothing. It was far too dangerous to sleep inside the life raft with the tide rising and lightening striking. The plane shaking, I searched for the first aid kit, finding it quickly, and grabbed some bottled water. Getting to my knees, I cleaned up her still bleeding wound below the sizeable bump on her head, applied some antibacterial ointment, and then covered it with an adhesive bandage. I then hurried to the cockpit to turn on the faulty engine so that we'd get some air and additionally turned on the landing lights to illuminate the aircraft—just in case anyone was looking for us. Fat chance in this storm. Then, I returned to my wife, taking a seat so I could cradle her head in my lap. And keep a hand on her heart to feel it beat. Never leaving her side except to pee or have a quick snack. I've lived on a diet of water, Chex Mix, and whiskey. And have hardly slept a wink.

As the storm continues to rage, my tiger still hasn't regained full consciousness. And to make matters worse, she's developed a high fever. Her forehead on fire, she's in some kind of delirium, hallucinating and having nightmares. Often she wakes up hysterical, crying out my name. Other times, she screams for our kids—Leo and Maeve. Nothing I do can comfort her. While I've tried to make her drink water whenever she's semi-conscious and swallow some Tylenol to bring down her scorching fever, I'm worried sick that she's not going to make it. And if she does, I wonder how bad her head injury is. Does she have brain damage? Amnesia? Will she remember me?

Tomorrow's our actual tenth anniversary, which happens to coincide with my birthday. My fortieth. Downing a shot of whiskey, I lower the window shade to block out the flashes of lightning. With a finger, I trace my sleeping wife's full lips—those gorgeous lips I couldn't resist when she asked me to kiss her on a dare. Those kissable lips that I hope will forever be mine. As another wave of gloom and doubt washes over me, I plant a chaste kiss on them and brush a strand of her matted hair out of her face, her soft skin still blazing beneath my touch. Then, I put the headphones of my iPod, which I'd stashed in my pocket before my jog, into my ears to block out the sound of the ruthless rain pounding the body of the unsteady plane as well as that of the gusting wind and the fierce waves crashing against it. And to block out all the dark thoughts that plague me. I feel like I'm in some kind of end-of-the-world movie. Or at least, the end of us.

We're running out of food and water.

We're running out of fuel.

We may never be rescued.

We may never see our family again.

My tiger may die.

We both may die.

And even if I survive, I don't think I could live without her. I love her too damn much.

Why hasn't anyone found us? Half delirious myself from being cooped up in this claustrophobic plane, my imagination goes wild.

The world's blown up.

We're under attack.

There's a World War.

We've been invaded by aliens. Little flesh-eating, Gumby-like green creatures with razor-sharp teeth creep into my mind. *Chomp! Chomp! Chomp!*

They've gotten our families. We're in an apocalypse.

Jen and I are the last two people left on Earth. On this island.

Except, she's going to die.

And it'll only be me.

Heart-pulsing rage surges inside me. I let out a roar. Raw, brazen, and loud like a savage. Born out of desperation. Primal need. From a place deep inside me I never knew I had.

Fuck. This. Shit.

It helps. I feel like I've unloaded. Like an explosive volcano. One erupting with hot, molten lava. My release taking hold of me, I find Jen's favorite song on my iPod.

Katy Perry's "Roar."

The song gives me a glimmer of hope. Huddled next to my sleeping beauty, I brush her warm cheeks with the back of my hand and hold her in my gaze. She's got the eye of the tiger. A fighter. As it fades out, I close my heavy eyelids.

And silently pray we'll make it through tomorrow.

There's nothing more I want for my birthday than to hear *my* tiger roar.

Chapter 16

Blake

DAY 7

I'm in a stupor. For a minute, I don't know where I am or what day it is. The haze doesn't last long and lifts quickly. Squeezing my eyes, I remember. It's December 21st. Both my fortieth birthday and tenth wedding anniversary. I've been trapped on a deserted island with my wife for a week in the middle of the Indian Ocean. And for the past few days, there's been some kind of motherfucker storm, maybe a monsoon, and I've been confined to the airplane I had to bring to an emergency landing, taking care of my gravely ill, injured wife. I blink my eyes open and gaze down at her. For the first time in days, she looks peaceful. Her breathing is even, and when I put my hand to her forehead, her skin is cool to my touch. Her fever's broken. Thank fucking God.

I fell asleep last night wearing earbuds and when I remove them, something is different. The rain's not pounding against the plane, and the aircraft is no longer shaking. I reach across Jennifer and lift the window shade an inch, not wanting to wake her from her sound sleep. A ray of sunshine peeks through the slit. The storm's died down.

With guarded optimism, I start my fortieth birthday with a trip to the toilet. Clad in my still damp board shorts, I do my morning business, taking a leak to get rid of my morning wood. Contemplating the day, I rake my hand through my unruly hair and then rub my hand across my thick beard. I must look like a fucking caveman. Having not shaved or bathed for seven days (except for some dips in the ocean), I'm not smelling like a rose. And that could be an understatement. Weather permitting, and of course, only if Jen is stable, maybe later today I'll get off this damn plane and take a dip in the ocean. Wash my hair. And put a razor to my face.

With a bottle of water in my hand, I return to my wife. And get an unexpected surprise. My tiger's awake and she's struggling to sit up. I rush to her side.

"Jen, let me help you!" Dropping the bottle on the floor, I circle my arms around her and get her into an upright position. Fixing the blanket around her, I notice how pale and thin she looks. Blinking her eyes, she also looks confused.

"Blake . . ." Her voice, a hoarse whisper, trails off as if hurts to talk.

Reaching down, I grab the water bottle. "Here, baby, drink some water." I hand her the bottle and she puts it to her soft lips, which I kept moist thanks to the first aid kit. She takes several gulps, one after another.

"Baby, drink slowly."

She takes one more sip and then asks, her voice stronger, "Blake, what are we doing on the plane? Are we going home?"

My heart stutters. I wish I could tell her we were, but instead I inform her that we're still on the island and weathered a major storm. "I think it was a monsoon. We've been on the plane for almost four days."

Her brows lift in surprise, and then she grimaces. Her head must hurt.

"How do you feel?" I ask.

"I'm hungry and I have a headache." She puts her hand to her forehead and rubs the bandage covering her gash. "Ow."

"Do you want me to get some Tylenol?"

"Maybe later. I'll live."

I'll live. The words swirl around in my head and I shudder inwardly. How close I was to losing her! But on my next heartbeat, I remind myself she's alive! My wife *is* going to live! Relief floods me. Lifting her hand away from her forehead, I tenderly kiss the bandaged spot. The bump above it is still there though it's considerably smaller.

"Do you remember what happened?"

She takes another sip of the water. "I remember getting lost in the rainforest in the middle of the storm. It was scary as hell."

Tell me. "Thank God, you left me a note. I went after you and found you unconscious and bleeding under a tree. I think a coconut fell on your head. You were practically comatose for three days."

She processes my words. "Three days?"

I nod. "Yeah, three fucking long days. You've had me worried shitless."

"Three days," she murmurs again. And then, the dimpled smile I know so well and love lifts her lips, melting away all my worries. Her emerald eyes light up.

"Happy Birthday, Blake!"

Those three words are the best present I could ever get. My heart swells with emotion. I flash a big smile back at her, holding back tears. I'm having a Doctor Phil moment. One escapes. Okay, call me a wuss. I can handle it.

"Happy Anniversary, baby!" I take her into my arms and hug her. How good it feels to hold her! To feel her heart beat against mine. Yes, my tiger's alive!

She runs her fingers through my hair and eyes me coyly. "A hug? Is that all I'm going to get on our tenth anniversary?"

"How about this?" On my next breath, I tug at her ponytail, coiling it around my hand, and tilt her head back. As she gasps, I press my mouth to hers and bite her upper lip, forcing them to part. The kiss is passionate and fierce. Just like our first. The blindfolded one. Two uninhibited mouths. Lips gnawing and sucking. Tongues tangoing. Bodies melting into each other. Breaths meshing. Moans mingling. Sparks flying. Colliding. I feel my cock swelling. Pulsing.

And then she puts her hand to my hot, hungry length. Stroking it. Loving it. Her mouth pulls away from mine. Her cheeks are flushed, her lips swollen, and she's breathless.

"Seriously, Blake, just a kiss? This is a milestone anniversary."

"Seriously, baby?" I can't believe she's up for it. Testosterone shoots through my man veins and blood rushes to my dick.

A few rapid heartbeats later, I'm seated next to her and she's straddling me. We're making slow, beautiful love. Every stroke measured and determined. Her pussy embracing my thrusting, rigid shaft. My hands gripping her tiny waist, supporting and guiding her, letting her determine the pace. Love and lust swirling around my brain, I kiss her everywhere I can, humming with pleasure. Overcome by gratitude. One-eyed Mr. Burns is wearing his happy face.

Welcome back, baby.

What a way to start off our special day!

I feel my balls constrict, her pussy contract. Her

body arches back as it convulses all around me. She breathes out my name as I chase her orgasm. Catching up to it in no time. Ecstasy! Oh, Jen, Oh, Jen, Oh, Jen.

Welcome to our new club.

You've heard of the mile high one?

Well, this is the mile below one.

And it rocks.

Happy Anniversary to us!

Chapter 17

Blake

Getting out of the plane is as much a blessing as it is heartbreak.

Upside: The sun is shining and the ocean is calm. Not a cloud in the sky. Picture postcard card perfect weather.

Downside: Our *glampsite* is gone and all our possessions have been washed away. Okay, let me rephrase. The life raft and all *my* possessions are gone. My dozen or so gazillion dollar bags filled with thousands of dollars worth of clothing and other stuff, including my iPhone, computer, grooming products and cigars. Amazingly, Jen's two cheapo bags I bought for her online are still there. Surveying the area, I hold my tiger's hand.

"All my stuff is gone," I groan.

"What did you expect? Louis Vuitton vs. Sponge-Bob? C'mon. No contest. My SpongeBob is a survivor and may even live around here. I don't think your frou-frou Louis ever set foot outside Paris. Hell-o!"

"Maybe some of my bags will wash back on shore."

"I highly doubt it. Look at the bright side, my love. Some poor old fisherman in India is peddling your luggage and your Armani wardrobe for a small fortune. Or wearing it. With the amount of clothes you had in your bags, you've probably outfitted an entire village, including the women.

My wife loves to wear my clothes, and I picture her wearing one of my three-times too big jackets over my boxer shorts. Truthfully, she makes a good point and the image of her in my menswear turns me on. My cock flexes as she continues.

"Baby, think about the loss as a philanthropic thing. You're changing lives. Making them better."

"Yup, that's me. Humanitarian Blake Burns. Changing people's lives one Armani T-shirt at a time."

Jen bursts into laughter at my deadpan humor. Her laughter is like music to my ears. How good it is to hear it again! It's infectious and I start laughing too.

Still laughing, I deposit a bag of supplies I snagged from the plane onto the sand. Jen squeezes my hand and coaxes me to sit down with her.

Clad in my two remaining items of clothing—my orange and blue striped board shorts and my Conquest Broadcasting hoodie—I lower my ass with hers onto the still damp sand, sitting with our knees curled up to our chests. We dig our toes into the tepid granules. Our laughter dies down. Holding hands, we peer into the horizon. The mellow waves roll, one after another, in our direction as if they're welcoming us back. The blazing sun beating down on us, we share a long stretch of silence. Jen breaks it.

"Baby, how are we going to celebrate your birthday and our anniversary?"

"I'm going to cook us a gourmet meal."

She surveys the area. Our campfire is gone along with my fishing pole. Her face is clouded with doubt.

"How are you going to do that?"

"I still have my Swiss Army knife and lighter." I reach into my pocket and show her the items.

"We'll build a new fire. There's probably a ton of debris along the beach from the storm we can use. I'm also sure I can find another long stick somewhere for a fishing pole."

"Just don't go into the rainforest."

"I won't." While the post-storm weather is glorious, and I don't really think it's dangerous, I agree to her wish. I think more about our celebration.

"Then, I'm going to order a Hansen's cake. Chocolate buttercream with raspberry filling." Legendary Hansen's in Beverly Hills has been my go-to birthday cake place for as long as I can remember.

"Ha-ha! Very funny! A mud pie with forty lit sticks is more like it."

"Plus one for good luck," I add.

Jen sighs. "Yeah, one for good luck. We could use

it."

I can detect the melancholy in her voice. We've been marooned on this island for a week now and with each passing hour, our chance of being rescued is diminishing. What's more our supplies are running out and won't last a lifetime. Not even another birthday. Let alone another month. Most worrisome of all is our water supply. We only have enough for a few more days. After that, we'll need another rainfall. And quite truthfully, I dread one. Instead of sharing my doom and gloom, I cheer Jen up.

"Baby, we *do* have good luck." I think back to our nuptials ten years ago. The day of my thirtieth birthday. With her unexpected hemorrhage in the middle of our ceremony, she was rushed to the hospital, and when I found out that she might have ovarian cancer, I freaked out and remembered that the one thing I wanted on my big three-oh was to wake up to my wife. To make Jennifer McCoy, Mrs. Blake Burns. To start the next decade with the girl I loved with my heart, my body, and my soul. Luck was on our side then and I need to believe that luck will be on our side now. That we will survive and spend the next decade together. And way more.

I turn toward Jen. She still looks wistful.

"Jen, baby. Think about all the luck we've had in our lives. You survived a cancer-scare. I survived Katrina. We had miracle babies when we thought we couldn't have any. They have two fantastic sets of grandparents. Plus Grandma and Luigi. We're successful. In great health. The plane didn't crash. I didn't get malaria. We survived the storm. And we're here. Together."

Turning her head, she meets my gaze. Her emerald eyes are teary. "Blake Burns, you're right. In fact, I'm the luckiest girl in the world. I have you. As my husband. My lover. The father of our children." She pauses, lifting my hand to her lips, pressing my knuckles against their softness. "And you're my hero. I love you so much."

"Tiger, I love you like crazy. You're the best thing that ever happened to me."

On my next breath, I cup her face and brush my lips across hers. The kiss is not my usual hot, fierce, and possessive kind. It's different. It's a softer kiss, one born of longing and apprehension. I can feel the aching on her lips too. Her need and fear. It's like a torch song. Hopeful and sad at the same time. We're on borrowed time. With my tongue, I deepen the kiss, letting her know that I'll be with her to the end of time. She'll always be mine. And I'll always be hers. She fully gives herself to me, her mouth and body melting into mine, and as I prolong the kiss, hope once again spills into my veins. We're meant to be lucky.

We spend the next half-hour reminiscing. While I no longer have my iPhone, Jen still has hers. It's in her backpack that's perched on the sand next to us. While we still can't get Wi-Fi, at least we can look at the gazillion photos I've archived on it.

Most of them are pictures we've taken of the kids with us and family members. Each brings back a special memory. Be it a birthday, a holiday, or a milestone like a first step or missing tooth. There are also videos of the kids—their first time on skis in Sun Valley, riding a bike without training wheels, singing Karaoke at my father's seventy-fifth birthday, doing the twist with Grandma and Luigi at my parents' fiftieth anniversary party, squealing on Disneyland rides, climbing up the Eiffel tower, and ripping open Christmas and Chanukah presents. Despite our hectic schedules, we've done so much together as a family. Leo and Maeve have given us so much joy. I love them as much as I love my wife. I'd die for them and I'd kill for them. Slay dragons if I had to.

"Do you think the kids are okay?" Jen asks as we view the array with a bittersweet mixture of fondness and sadness in our hearts.

"Totally. I'm sure our parents are keeping them busy and have figured out a way for them not to worry."

"Do you think our folks think we're dead?"

"No. My father's an eternal optimist and someone who's succeeded by always doing the impossible. Trust me, he hasn't stopped looking for us, and he won't until we're found."

Jen chews her bottom lip, not totally buying my words. Before she can challenge me or express her doubts, I make her look at more photos and videos. We go back ten years and view all of them from our Christmas in July wedding, as we fondly refer to it. The one I secretly planned at her parents' house, complete with fake snow and a live performance by Roberta Flack who sang our song.

"That was our most fun wedding." We actually had three weddings. Believe me, it's complicated. Someone could write a book about them.

"Yeah, it was the most fun, but it's not my favorite."

My brow lifts and my ego deflates a little. "Seriously, babe? I put so much time and effort into it. It wasn't easy keeping it secret and you blindfolded."

"And handcuffed," she adds with a roll of her eyes.

"Yeah, that wasn't good." Stupid me lost the key and had to schlep through a damn Wal-Mart to get them off. Nope, that part wasn't fun. "So, which was your fave?"

She smiles. "The one at the hospital. After my surgery."

"With that pothead minister?"

My tiger laughs. "Yeah, Reverend Dooby! And with those SpongeBob Band-Aids you used for wedding bands. That was so creative, Blake."

My ego inflates. I flash a Cheshire cat grin. "Thanks, baby. Talking about Band-Aids, I should take a look at your cut. Hold still." I rip off the bandage on her forehead and she winces.

"How does it look?"

"Pretty good. It's closed up. But it may leave a scar."

Jen makes a face.

"Don't worry, Calamity. I love your scars. All of them. They make you special. Show you've survived." I trace a finger along the biggest. The six-inch one on her abdomen left behind from her surgery. The one that bothers her the most, though for me, it's the one I love more than any other. It's the one that affirmed my love for her. My desire to love her, cherish her, and protect her forever.

"You're tickling me, Blake!" Lolling her head back at my touch, Jen giggles. "You know why that wedding was my favorite?"

I stop tickling her. "No, tell me."

Her gaze meets mine again, holding me lovingly. "Because you said your forever vows to me knowing that my days might be numbered. That you loved me unconditionally and were truly committed to me until death do us part."

"Aww, baby. Nothing's changed." I flash back to that moment and remember holding her frail body in my arms, loving her more than she could ever know.

Connected to her mind, body, and soul. Knowing right then and there she was the only woman I'd ever want to spend my life with. No matter how much time we had together or not. Reverently, I take her left hand, and lifting it to my lips, I kiss her snowflake diamond ring. The one I surprised her with inside a snow globe before proposing on one knee. As I release my lips, the sun hits the center stone and it glistens in my eyes.

When I set her hand down, she squints into the horizon. "Blake, do you ever think about having more children?"

"Yeah, sometimes. But I'm perfectly happy with the two we have. I love them to pieces."

"Should we try for a third if we make it home?"

"You mean like get another surrogate?" On account of her partial hysterectomy, my tiger's unable to bear children. Let me rephrase, unable to carry them. Using Jen's eggs, we had our son and daughter via in vitro fertilization and surrogates—my sister Marcy for Leo and Jen's best friend Libby for Maeve. It's unlikely either would carry for us again nor would we ask them.

Jen shakes her head. "No, I'm thinking we should adopt. It would be a way of giving back if we survive this island and make it back home alive."

"Baby, I'm game. I like that idea." Yup, call me the gift that keeps on giving. Then, I'm reminded. A sudden pang of guilt and regret stabs me. I don't have an anniversary gift for my wife. Not a single one. They floated away with my luggage. Along with the card I had custom made. Inside it was the poem I recited to her when we got married for the third time in July. My personal wedding vow.

"Baby, bad news."

Jen looks at me alarmed. "What?"

"I don't have an anniversary gift to give you. I'm sorry. It was in one of my bags."

Relief colors her face. "What was it?"

"I don't know if I should tell you."

"C'mon, tell me."

"You know how you've never believed I was a Boy Scout?"

"Mr. Born with a Silver Spoon in Your Mouth, you couldn't have possibly been one."

"Well, baby, I really was. And to prove it, I asked my mother to dig up my merit medal as well as the photo of me getting it. It was perfect because the medal was aluminum—it's what I read online is traditional for tenth anniversaries. I had the medal re-set in a gold border with ten diamonds so you could wear it as a pin or pendant, and the photo framed for you to put on your desk."

"Seriously, Blake?"

"Yeah, Scout's Honor. You can ask my mother."

Jen's expression softens. "I believe you, my love. That is the sweetest thing ever."

"I'm sorry I can't give it to you."

And another gift as well. One I'm not going to tell my wife about. Nor the card. When we get back home, I'll have them duplicated. That is, *if* we get back home. Doubt creeps back into my bloodstream. It's hard to keep it at bay.

"Well, some fisherman in India has a nice Christmas present for his wife," says my tiger before I can sulk.

I laugh. I love my wife's sense of humor. The way she can always make me feel better. And in more ways than one. "And, that dude's probably wondering who's that kid with the braces in that dork uniform with all the weird badges."

"Blake, you were never a dork. That I *do* know for sure."

I laugh harder. Yup, she's right. Blake Burns was never a dork. I take my wife into my arms and position her on my lap. Her legs straddle me. I tuck a loose strand of her hair behind her ear and then stroke her jaw with my thumb.

"Baby, I'll make it up to you when we get back home."

"Blake, my love, you don't have to get me anything. You are my gift. And except for being reunited with our family, the only thing I could ever want. Or hope for." Her eyes burn into mine as a seductive smile plays on her lips.

"Fuck me."

The best two words a man can hear from the woman he loves. Happy Birthday to me!

Before I know it, we're bared to each, fucking our brains out on the shimmering sand as the scorching sun shines above us. Our heated bodies perfectly synched. Our hot breaths almost one. Bucking and thrusting until we come. It never ceases to amaze me that after ten years of marriage we still have this effect on each other. It just keeps getting better. We can't get enough of each other. I know every inch of her body, exactly how she likes it. How she wants it. And like me, she knows what I want. What I need. What I love. God, how I love and adore my tiger.

Her muscles clenching around me, Mr. Burns picks up his tempo. Thrusting harder and faster. Bringing us closer to the edge. Then with a carnal grunt, I explode as a scream of my name pours out of her luscious mouth and she vibrates like a timber drum all around me.

Maybe our simultaneous orgasms can't get us off this island, but they take us into space.

Chapter 18

Jennifer

After our delicious fuck, we jump into the ocean for a quick dip and return to our ravished site. My turn to give Blake his anniversary present as well as his birthday present.

Blake's right. Traditionally, the tenth year of marriage is symbolized by aluminum—or tin. Both materials represent the durability and flexibility needed to sustain a loving union. Trust me, being married to someone as outrageous and high maintenance as Blake requires a lot of flexibility. I suppose it's one of the reasons we're trapped on this island. I'm after all the one who let him fly us here. In retrospect, what was I thinking? On the other hand, maybe this is a test of our durability. Our strength as a couple. An empowering experience. Blake eyes me sheepishly and cuts into my thoughts.

"Tiger, I feel guilty taking these presents."

I'm holding two gift-wrapped boxes in my arms. Eager to give them to him.

"Don't be, my love. With all your luggage gone, you need a few new things."

I hand him the first present. I'm super excited about it. It's a vintage tin box I found at the Santa Monica flea market—Blake collects boxes—and inside it I've put ten Cuban Montecristo No. 4 cigars. My husband's only real vice—other than me. He explained to me once why he loves them. "Smoking cigars is like falling in love. First, you're attracted by its shape; you stay for its flavor, and you must always remember never, never to let the flame go out."

"Open it!" I watch eagerly as Blake tears off the paper. His sapphire eyes brighten.

"Wow! This is a cool box."

"It's tin—the other material that commemorates the ten-year mark." My eyes don't blink as he examines the slightly dinged box. It's an old advertising tin for Muriel Senators, a popular brand of cigars that are still made.

"Ha! My grandma's name!"

"That's one of the reasons it appealed to me. Now open it."

My gaze stays fixed on him as he lifts off the lid. His eyes growing wide, he's like a kid in a candy store.

"Wow! Montecristos! My favorites!" He sniffs the cigars and then smacks a kiss on my lips. "I LOVE you, tiger!"

I'm feeling super-proud of myself. I secretly bought

the authentic Cuban cigars in Aruba while we were there with the kids at his parents' vacation house last summer. He wastes no time lighting one up. He puts it to his mouth and inhales it before exhaling a puff of smoke.

It took me a while to get used to the smell, but now I don't mind it. In fact, one of the sexiest things about Blake is the way he smokes a cigar. The way he warms it in his hands, lights it up, holds it between his fingers, and sucks on it with gusto. It's a total turn-on. My body is buzzing all over as he takes another long, satisfying draw, his eyes half-closing from the extreme pleasure.

"Okay, now open your birthday present."

Sliding the lit cigar to the side of his mouth, Blake sets the tin on the sand and then takes his other present from me. He rips off the bow and paper. The shiny white box beneath the wrapping is from Neiman Marcus. Or Needless Markup as I like to call it. One of Blake's favorite stores.

He grins. "This has got to be good."

My eyes remain on him as he pops off the lid and peels away the neatly folded layer of tissue paper covering the contents.

Again, his eyes light up and he flashes a big smile.

"Tiger! I love it!"

"Happy Birthday, baby!" I've given him a Turnbull and Asser blue and white striped dress shirt and a coordinating silk tie. Blake loves it when I pick out his shirts and ties. He only has about three hundred of each. What's one more?

"I'm going to be the best dressed man on this island!"

"Baby, you're going to be the *only* dressed man on this island." I add that the shirt will also provide lightweight mosquito protection. I never told him how much I worried that he might come down with a deadly disease from all those mosquito bites. The fleeting thought makes me shudder.

Laughing his sexy laugh, he holds up the jacquard tie. "This tie is awesome. There's a lot of things I can do with it." His eyes twinkle with a wicked glint.

"Blake, are you implying that you want to tie me up?"

He affectionately flicks my nose. "I'm thinking about it, tiger."

Hot tingles rush to my core. My skin prickles. The thought of kinky sex with Blake is always a turn on. On my next heated breath, he grabs my wrists and binds them with the tie behind my back. Giggling, I try to wriggle myself free, but it's futile.

"Get used to my tie. You'll be wearing it all day."

"Seriously?"

"Seriously. Think of it as my anniversary present to you. You'll be thanking me later."

"I'm not going to be very useful to you this way. I mean, I can't help you gather bark, make a fire, or cook dinner."

He smirks. "Don't worry, you'll be plenty useful to me."

Another set of flutters gathers between my thighs. I'm as wet as the ocean. As hot as the sun. "Are you going to fuck me again, Blake?"

"Not yet. You need something else way more first."

A good spanking?

He tugs at my matted, knotty ponytail and winks.

"A good shampooing."

Chapter 19

Jennifer

1. Oral Sex: The man you love licking your pussy.

2. Procreation: The man you love fucking you senseless.

3. Kissing: The man you love fucking your mouth with his tongue.

4. Massage: The man you love giving you a rub-down.

5. Shampoo: The man you love massaging your scalp.

Blake is pure genius at all these things. An expert. And they're equally sensuous. Depending on my needs and mood, I sometimes want one more than the others. Right now, there's nothing more I want than a fabulous shampoo. It's been seven long days since I've washed my hair. From the salty sea, humidity, sand, monsoon, and my fever, it's matted, knotty, dirty, and sticky. My scalp itches. For all I know, there are some creepy bugs crawling around it, but I banish that icky thought when Blake squirts a dollop of my shampoo onto my hair and begins to work my scalp, lathering it with his deft fingers. Bared to each other, we're standing thigh deep in the ocean. Given our limited water supply, we made a compromise to wash my hair with the salty seawater and rinse it off with a bottle of our Evian.

My back to his chest, I hear Blake inhale. "Baby, I love the smell of your shampoo."

It's Gloria's Secret's Very Cherry Vanilla. I've been using it forever. Careful to avoid both my gash and bump, he digs his fingertips deeper into my scalp. Circling and scrubbing. The physical sensation combined with the squishy sound arouses me. And so does the intoxicating scent of the sea mixing with the fruity cleanser. Relaxing every muscle in my body like aromatherapy. Surrendering myself to him, I hum a contented *Mmm.* Then sigh. Sheer ecstasy.

"God, Blake, this feels so incredible." I tilt back my head, my spine arching, my tied-up hands skimming the warm water behind me. His erection presses against me. He's as turned on as I am. My flesh prickles with heat while my pussy tickles with need. I have the burning desire to touch myself there and silently curse not having my hands accessible.

"Blake, would you mind untying my hands?" My voice is syrupy sweet.

"Later, baby." I detect the amusement in his voice. "I'm not done here."

As I read into his words, he applies the conditioner

and afterward rinses off my hair with the purified water. Then, he puts his nose to my scalp. Inhaling me, he moans loudly on the exhale.

"Fuck, baby. I've got to have you."

No need to beg. Before I can take my next breath, he cinches my waist and takes me from behind. Somehow managing to get his cock inside, pounding me until we both come in the water despite my tightly bound hands.

Like I said, the man's pure genius.

Chapter 20

Jennifer

I'll do anything to get my hands untied.

Though the ruggedness turns me on, I offer to shave Blake's caveman beard. No dice.

I offer to give him a massage. No dice.

I offer to give him a hand job. No dice. He says he'd rather have a blowjob. Though when I offer to suck him off, no dice.

The bottom line, my husband is enjoying every minute of having me tied up. With no TV on the island, I guess it's his form of entertainment. A snarky smile forms on his delicious lips every time I ask him to take off the tie or find myself unable to do something as simple as taking a sip of water, putting my hair up in a ponytail, or tying the string of my bikini top.

Frustration mounts. It gets to the point of begging. "Please, Blake, take off the tie . . . pretty please? With a cherry on top?"

My husband loves when I beg. It turns him on. My begging only entertains him more. I beg and I beg and I beg. But it's hopeless. I have to resign myself to the fact that he's going to spend the rest of our anniversary with a perpetual hard-on and a smug smirk on his face.

We end the day by taking a long walk on the beach looking for materials to rebuild our campfire and Blake's fishing pole. Blake's carrying my tote and smoking a cigar. In the aftermath of the storm, we find tons of bark and seashells plus another long, sturdy stick for a new fishing pole.

"What are you going to use for a hook?" I ask on our way back. With his bags washed away, a wire hanger is no longer a possibility.

He takes a puff of his half-smoked cigar. "We're going to have to resort to your dangling earrings."

"Great! Let me look for them." Another ploy to get my hands untied. I tug at the silk fastening. Nothing gives.

Blowing out a ring of smoke, Blake wraps his arm around me. "Nice try, tiger. Nothing doing."

When we get back to our spot on the beach, I have to endure the humiliation of him riffling through my bag. More specifically, through the silk mesh bag in which I've packed all my lingerie and the earrings.

He holds up one of my lacy bras. A red one. "Tiger, this is a nice one. When did you get it?"

"It's part of that collection of Gloria's Secret lingerie you had Gloria send me that first New Year's we spent together. At their beach house."

"Right." He twists his lips. I wonder if he's thinking the same thing I am—the New Year's we broke up when I discovered he'd masterminded my break up with my fiancé. Which later I came to never regret.

Thought confirmed. "We're going to burn it." He tosses it onto the sand. He dips his hand back into the lingerie bag. "Where are these from?" He examines a sexy black garter with little bows and a package of sheer black lace-trimmed stockings. His suspicious eyes narrow. "Hmm. I don't remember buying you these."

I feel myself cringing. "Um, I bought them. I was going to put them on for you tonight . . . surprise you in our suite at The Ritz . . . and wear the little black dress I brought along."

A slow, devilish smile burns on his face. "I think I'm going to have to dress you up in them tonight for dinner."

"Blake, the garters are very hard to hook." Hint Hint: Untie my hands.

"Don't worry, baby. I'm very handy."

I flash him a fuck-you smile. He shoots a cocky one back at me. Sometimes, it's infuriating being married to him.

He continues to rummage through my lingerie, adding a black lace push-up bra and matching thong to my anniversary ensemble. Growing irritable, I hope he finds the earrings soon. Instead, he pulls out a purple satin drawstring bag and holds it up.

"What's this?"

Shit. I totally forgot I packed this. Mortification heats my skin. I feel my cheeks flare.

"Um, uh, it's just something Libby gave me to celebrate our tenth anniversary." My kinky best friend somehow ended up with two of these lovelies and bestowed me with the extra one.

"Hmm. Thoughtful of her." My eyes stay on him as he loosens the pouch and dips his hand inside it. He slides out a small shiny stainless steel object. J-shaped, it's a hook with a ball and chain that has a small loop at the end. His eyes widen.

"Seriously, babe. She gave us a fishing hook? How could you not have told me earlier?"

I twist my mouth, making stuttering noises and excuses as he plucks his hand back into the purple sack.

He pulls out the folded up instructions, and as he silently reads them, his eyes gleam deviously, and a wry smile curls his lips. He's discovered it's no ordinary hook. But rather a sex toy to insert up my butt.

"Tiger, it's time to put all that Scout training to good use."

Less than five minutes later, I'm lubed up with some gel I brought along and the ball portion of the hook is so far high up my butt I feel like I'm going to choke on it. While I've had plenty of backdoor play with Blake, this feels different and it takes a bit of getting used to. But because the metal is warm, not cold, on account of the tropical weather, I quickly grow acclimated to it. Following suggestions from the instruction pamphlet, Blake has knotted a cluster of my long, clean hair around the loop so I can only move in a limited number of positions. I can't bend forward or stand up or I'll painfully pull out a chunk of my mane. So, I'm stuck on my knees on the sand, and gripping my haunches, he's fucking my ass. With every deep thrust, the ball presses against my cervix, the pressure tantalizing my nerve endings, the stimulation so intense I want to jump out of my skin. Even the smallest movement reverberates inside me. Having my hair tied to the hook and my hands tied behind my back, I can only submit. Resistance is futile. I'm helpless and loving it. Totally hooked!

"Baby, this is the best tackle I've ever encountered." In my mind's eyes, I can picture my husband's lips twisting into a fiendish grin as he fucks me senseless. "Just call me Captain Hook."

Moments later, a different kind of monsoon crashes through my body, taking every cell and molecule of my being as a tidal wave of euphoria spreads through my core. My toes curl in the sand as I gasp out my release. With a savage grunt, Blake's release follows mine, his hot cum spilling into to me, some pouring down the back of my thighs.

Recovering, he pulls out of me and frees my hair with a slash of his Swiss Army knife—adieu dead ends—and removes the hook. Oddly enough, I feel bereft without it.

"Wow! This is amazing!"

I reposition myself, kneeling so that I face him.

"What's amazing, Captain Hook?" *Or was.*

He holds out his palm. Capturing the sunlight, the glistening hook is in his hand, but the ball has fallen off and jitters beside it.

"The ball's detachable." Tossing the ball onto the sand, he exams the hook, now with its rough edge, and I'm silently grateful the ball didn't fall off while inside me because that would have hurt like hell.

"This is the perfect fishing hook. And the fish are going to love the taste of you, tiger."

I watch as he reassembles a fishing pole, using the stick we found, my dental floss, the hook, and a fan-shaped shell from our collection as a weight, thanks to a small pinprick-size hole. Finally, he adds a gummy worm as a lure. Honestly, he *is* handy. Thanks to his Boy Scout days? I just don't understand why he can't hang a picture on a wall at home or change a light bulb.

Wearing his board shorts and his iPod wrapped around his bicep, his pole in hand, he heads toward the ocean. I follow him but tell him I'll watch him from the shore. I don't want to get my newly shampooed hair all wet and messed up. Cascading over my shoulders and already sun-dried, it feels so good to have my mane at last silky and clean.

Holding the pole up, he struggles to put his earbuds in his ears.

"Want me to hold it for you? Or put in your earbuds?" My voice is as sweet as sugar. Another opportunity to get my hands untied. It's not exactly comfortable having them stuck behind my back. My shoulders ache.

Another smug smirk. "Sheesh, baby, you really are persistent. What part of I'm-not-taking-the-tie-off don't you get?" He chuckles.

It's not funny! As I scrunch my face in frustration, he starts wading into the water.

"Wish me good luck, baby!" he calls out, looking over his shoulder.

Simmering, I narrow my eyes at him. Then impulsively, I poke out my tongue, making the obnoxious throaty sound my kids make when they do that. At least, I'm not tongue tied, no pun intended. My action backfires and instead gets a rise out of him. He blows me a kiss with his lush lips. My beautiful bastard!

Resigning myself to my situation, my gaze stays on him as he heads out deeper and deeper. I can't help but smile at the sight of him. While nothing can compare to his gorgeous face, his broad, tanned, sculpted back is like eye candy. Any way you look at him, my husband is sexy as sin. A bronzed god. I can't wait for him to come back, and I start fantasizing about having more kinky sex with him. Wearing the black garter and stockings, my legs spread in the air as I lie on the white shimmering sand while he ravages me. Somehow, he's managed to keep my mind off our terrible fate on our special day. Though I long to be home, there could be way worse things than being stranded with Blake Burns on a deserted island.

Chest-deep, Blake's been in the water for about twenty minutes without a single bite when I see it in the near distance to the right. A giant fin is sticking out of the water. Oh my God!! A shark! And it's heading Blake's way at turbo speed!

My heart leaps to my throat as panic seizes me. "Blake, Blake! Get out of the water!" I shout out at the top of my lungs. Shit! With his earbuds plugged in, he can't hear me.

I run into the ocean, still yelling out his name. Wishing I could use my arms to propel myself faster. Frantically, with that horrific opening scene from *Jaws* in my head, I slosh through the water. Halfway to him, my thighs burning and out of breath, I gasp and lose my footing when . . .

Chapter 21

Blake

B alls. Why isn't one biting? I've been standing chest-deep in this ocean for almost a half-hour waiting for a taker, but so far *nada*. Maybe the monsoon or whatever the hell it was sent the fish away. Or they've lost their taste for gummy worms. I'm losing my patience. Anyone will tell you, patience isn't one of my virtues.

Suddenly, a few feet in front of me a humongous slate creature leaps out of the water. Startled and the splash so forceful when it dives back into the sea, I lose my balance and fall backward into the water, my whole body going under. I get my bearings, stand up, only to have the same encounter again. This time in the reverse direction. But this time I stay on my feet.

It's a dolphin. A beautiful bottlenose gray dolphin! And it's flirting with me!

Both my iPod shuffle and earbuds are waterproof, but the latter have fallen out of my ears. As the showoff dolphin does a twist in the air, I attempt to reinsert them, but am stopped by a scream. A garbled, dire scream of my name, so familiar.

"Blake!"

My heart pounding, I spin around. My eyes widen and panic grips me. Jesus! It's my wife. Jen, floundering in the over-her-head water. An undertow! She's drowning! My eyes meet her desperate ones.

"Blake!" she cries out again, her voice hoarse. Shit! She can't paddle toward me with her hands tied up. Oh, God. What have I done?

"Hang on, baby!" I cry out. I let go of my pole, guilt swimming in my veins as I swim to her as fast as I can. Stroking and kicking so hard you'd think I was competing in the Olympics.

On a breath, I watch her go under again. Fear fills every atom of my being when she doesn't resurface. I swim faster, my limbs in high gear, battling the current.

Her head crashes through the water again. Gasping for air, she hoarsely calls out my name once more and then gets swept back under.

"Jen!" I cry out on another breath. I stroke my arms faster, kick my legs harder, calling on every ounce of muscle power I have. My body's a machine. Breathless, I reach her just as she resurfaces. She's choking—coughing and spitting up water. And sobbing.

Grabbing her, I anchor her so she's upright and facing me. "I've got you, baby."

Even though she's safe with me, she grows more

hysterical. Her sobs are gutting me. Jesus! She almost drowned! Despite living by the ocean and having a pool in our yard, my Boise born and bred wife has never become a strong swimmer.

I hold her in my arms as she wraps her legs around me. I feel guilty as sin that I tied up her hands. My gut-wrenching guilt morphs into unbearable self-loathing when I think I almost lost her. Once again. And this time it was my fault. All my fault. I feel like I've been punched in the stomach. Stupid, stupid me.

"Shh." I hush her, kissing her neck. "Everything's okay."

Nothing I do or say can calm her down.

"Baby," she splutters through her tears, "I thought it was a shark. That your life was over . . . I was going to lose you."

"It was just a playful dolphin," I say in a soft calm, soothing voice, kissing her forehead, painfully aware of how much I mean to her. She loves me as much I love her, maybe more if more is possible though I doubt it. I push her wet strands of hair off her face. "I bet it'll come back tomorrow and bring a friend to play with us."

Thinking these words will end her sobs and hysteria, I'm wrong. So fucking wrong. She grows more hysterical, her heart-wrenching sobs uncontrollable, her pale pink lips trembling. She shakes her head back and forth as tears pour down her cheeks and her shoulders heave. Her face reddens as her watering, long lashed eyes sear into mine.

"No, Blake! I don't want a tomorrow here! I don't want to play with dolphins! I can't take this anymore! I want to be home! With our family! And play with our children!"

Her eyes flooding with despair and her nose running, she continues to splutter. "We promised we'd be back by Christmas. To celebrate Maeve's birthday. Open presents under the tree. But we won't, Blake. No, we won't!"

Her sobs pierce my chest, rip me apart, tear at my heart. She's fucking killing me. Christmas. The holiday that means the most to us. One that we both celebrate despite our religious differences and rightfully so. In addition to it to being our princess's birthday, it was at the Conquest Broadcasting Christmas party that I kissed my tiger under the mistletoe and she discovered I was *that* man who'd kissed her senseless at her engagement party. The night she gave her body to me, and I almost lost her from my reckless need and desire. Then, that Christmas Eve, I realized how much I loved her and traveled to her parents' house in a dire blizzard, risking my life, to tell her how I felt. She felt the same way. My heart sung with me: *All I want for Christmas is you.* One Christmas later, she was battling for her life and she was still all I wanted, and thank God, she came home wedded to me, healthy, our life full of promise and joy. Then our Christmas in July wedding at her parents' house, the one I surprised her with. A forever. Then, five years later on Christmas day our precious princess was born. Joining us and our beloved son, Leo. The events flash through my head like a PowerPoint presentation. Except at each slide I feel my power waning. Each cherished memory eating at my splintering heart, chewing one piece of it at a time. My tiger continues to cry, her sobs, like kryptonite, sucking everything out of me.

Holding her tightly, her legs twined around me, clinging to me like I'm a lifesaver, I say nothing. Knowing anything I say won't matter. As I carry her back to shore, she rests her head on my shoulder and weeps.

Silently, I weep with her.

For us.

For our kids.

For our family.

And for the good life we may never have again.

It takes all I have not to fall apart.

Chapter 22

Blake

I feel as gutted as a fish. As glum as an oyster. As spineless as a jellyfish. I was supposed to be my wife's superhero, but I can't fly her home or give her what she wants most. Fuck. I can't even protect her. Inwardly, I shudder thinking about how close I just came again to losing her. Hell. I can't even give her a beautiful tenth anniversary meal. We were supposed to be at the Ritz Carlton having a couple's massage followed by a gourmet eight-course dinner with flowing champagne in our own private villa on the beach. But now, we'll be lucky if we have a couple of granola bars or bags of chips and wash it all down with a couple of warm beers. As I step onto shore, a sudden sharp pain on the sole of my foot cuts into my rueful thoughts.

"OW!"

"What's the matter, Blake?" asks Jen as I jolt. Her first words to me since I rescued her.

Still carrying her, I look down. By my feet is a huge reddish crab, its pinchers still snapping at me. An idea comes to me. It's payback time! The little fucker is going to be dinner. I set Jen down so I can pick it up. As I carefully gather the nasty crustacean, hoping it won't snap at me again, Jen's eyes travel to the right.

"Blake, look!" Holding the crab between my thumb and index finger, I follow her gaze.

"Holy shit! It's the Boy Scout medal!" The diamond border glimmers in the sun. "I can't believe it washed up on shore."

Bending down, I scoop it up in my other hand.

Only minutes ago, I was a few breaths away from becoming totally unhinged. Things are looking up. A smile dances across my face as I clutch the medal.

"Happy Anniversary, baby!"

Chapter 23

Jennifer

Somehow the discovery of Blake's Boy Scout medal has lifted my spirits. A glimmer of hope flickers inside me. That we won't be on this island forever. That we'll be rescued soon and be reunited with our family. In time for Christmas. With renewed optimism, I decide to make the best of our special day.

"Baby, let me put this on you," my husband of ten years says, placing the diamond-encrusted medal around my neck. Unfortunately, the gold chain is missing, but clever Blake has created a makeshift one using my dental floss. He ties a knot behind my neck, the warm touch of his hands on my skin giving me goosebumps.

"This looks good on you, tiger." He admires his handiwork. "The jeweler did a great job adding the diamond border." I gaze down to where the pendant hits. Just above my cleavage.

"I love it, Blake. Thank you."

He plays with it, sliding it up and down my sensitive chest. "I love you, tiger. I'm glad I could give it to you after all. I wish I could have shown you the photo of me getting it, but that's likely shark chum now."

"Blake's let's not talk about sharks." For a second, I think back to my recent scare and shudder, but quickly shove the thoughts of losing Blake and drowning to the back of my mind.

Blake takes me into his arms. He's wearing the dress shirt I gave him. It's unbuttoned and the sleeves are rolled up, revealing both his sexy chiseled chest and forearms. The soft Egyptian cotton feels delicious against my skin. He nuzzles my neck.

"I wish I could give you more, baby. Grant you all your wishes like a genie."

I wiggle my hands, which are still tied up behind me. "Blake, there *is* something you can do. Untie my hands. Especially if you want me to put on that special outfit." My eyes dart to the black bra, thong, garter, and package of stockings. To my relief, he circles behind me and I can feel him working on the knot.

"Sorry, baby."

I'm not sure if he means he's sorry he tied me up or sorry he's waited so long to untie me.

"Shit!"

"What's the matter?"

"I can't undo the knot. It's too tight. Maybe when it dries out, I can undo it."

"Use your Swiss Army knife, Mr. Boy Scout."

"Good idea, babe."

"Shit."

"Now, what's wrong?" I scrunch my brows. Why don't I have a good feeling about where things are going?

"I lost my knife. It must have fallen out of my pocket in the ocean."

Though I rarely curse out loud, it's my turn to say shit. "Jesus, Blake, I can't put any clothes on . . ."

"That's *not* a problem."

"I can't feed myself."

"I'll feed you, baby."

"I can't touch you or hold you . . ."

"Yeah, that is a bit of a problem . . . but it could be a good one."

On my next exasperated breath, I'm flat on my back, my bound hands folded under my butt. Blake is on his knees. He spreads my legs.

"Bend your knees," he orders as he crawls between them. "I thought I'd have myself a delectable appetizer before I cooked Mr. Crab."

Oh, sweet Jesus! Is he going to do what I think he's going to do? When he buries his head between my legs and his mouth beelines for my pussy, I have my answer.

"Mmm. You taste delicious, my tiger," he murmurs as he goes down on me with a loud, wet succulent kiss. He then flicks his tongue on my clit, intermittently licking and sucking, his beard grazing my inner thighs and heightening my sensations. My back arches from the rush of pleasure and pain he's giving me, both equally delicious, equally intense. Writhing, my hands digging into my back, I begin to whimper.

"Blake, I'm going to come!" I cry out as my body builds toward climax, my muscles contracting, my heart pounding, my breaths coming out in desperate pants.

"Not until I'm inside you," he growls, repositioning himself so he's hovering over me, his hands planted on either side of my body.

"Take me, Blake! Please take me!" My need is so great, I want to implode.

"I love it when you beg, tiger. Now, I want to hear you roar. Roar so loud they hear you in California."

I watch as Blake buries his colossal cock in my entrance. Because I'm so wet and ready for him, it glides in effortlessly and fills me quickly. He begins to pummel me, thrusting in and out of me without mercy like a madman. His breathing ragged, he picks up his pace, hitting my G-spot over and over, his hot, rigid length heating my clit, bringing me closer and closer to the edge. My whimpers morph into sobs as waves of ecstasy begin to crash through me. I squeeze my eyes shut wishing I had use of my hands. Desperately needing something to hold on to. I ache to dig my nails into his skin. Or fist his hair with my fingers or ball the fabric of his shirt. His breathing grows harsher, his thrusts faster and more forceful. Our breaths mingle, his grunts meet my sobs, and then suddenly a new sound enters the mix. A choppy sound so familiar I want to cry. *Chup. Chup. Chup. Chup.* As I'm about to come, my eyes spring open and I look up at the sky. Hovering above us is a helicopter, its blades whirling.

"Oh my God!" I cry out, unsure if I orgasmed from pure physical ecstasy or the glorious sight above. "Blake, look!" So in the moment, I can't believe he hasn't noticed. Without stopping his machinations, he gazes up into the sky.

"Holy Shit! I can't believe it!"

My body in turmoil, he slides out of me and I sit up. He leaps to his feet, his mega-big cock still rigid. At full attention.

"U.S. Coast Guard," calls a husky voice from the chopper. "Mr. and Mrs. Blake Burns?"

"Yes!" Blake shouts back, cupping his hands to his mouth like a megaphone. Then, I hear him curse under his breath. In a panic, he yanks off his shirt and covers his huge erection. I don't know whether to laugh or cry. Either way there are tears of joy and relief in my eyes. We've been rescued! Whoo Hoo! Tying his shirt around his waist, my husband lifts me to my feet—I'm totally naked—and spins me around and around as the chopper descends. As it lands, he sets me down and smacks a hot kiss on my lips.

"Tiger, I think we're going to have to finish what we started at home."

Chapter 24

Jennifer

DAY 8

Twenty-four hours later we're back home. Because of the twelve-hour time difference, it's still December 21st in Los Angeles. The time: 10 p.m. Technically, it's still our anniversary and Blake's birthday.

The flight home was smooth. After a stop in Malé to get medical checkups, much needed showers, a good meal, some proper clothing for Blake as well as a shave plus some presents for the kids, we boarded a chartered-jet—courtesy of his father—at the airport. We learned earlier from authorities that because of the life-threatening monsoons sweeping the Maldives the entire week, it was virtually impossible to do an ongoing search and rescue mission. With the death toll at a hundred, many hospitalized, and others missing, we were lucky we survived. The private jet made one stop in Paris to refuel, and for the rest of the ten-hour flight,

I slept in Blake's arms. Excited but exhausted, he slept too.

My heart thuds against my chest as I ring the front door bell. Neither of us has house keys as I didn't bring any and Blake's washed away. Clad in jeans and a gray hoodie just like I am, Blake stands beside me and squeezes my hand.

The door swings open quickly. It's my mother with tears brimming in her eyes.

"Oh honey!" She gives me a big hug. "I'm so happy you're home. I was worried to death and thought I'd never see you again."

My beloved mom looks worse than I do. The poor woman looks like she hasn't slept for days and has aged years from worry. Her eyes are bloodshot and dark circles surround them. And several grays have sprouted in her ash-brown hair.

"Hi, Meg," chimes in Blake as if he's the neighborhood Pizza Hut delivery guy.

My mom gives Blake a hug as well. "Oh, Blake, it's so good to see you too."

She steps back and studies me. Alarm washes over her face.

"Oh, dear Lord, what happened to your head?" Her eyes zero in on the gash on my forehead, which the medics re-covered with a bandage.

"Mom, don't worry. It's just a little scratch. I'm perfectly fine." I spare her the gory details of being trapped in a rainforest in the middle of a monsoon.

"You sure?" My mother is such a worrier. Always has been.

"Trust me, Meg," pipes Blake. "She's perfectly fine."

My father joins my mother at the front door. His eyes light up at the sight of me. While he looks tired, he doesn't look half as haggard as my mom.

"Dad!" I wrap my arms around him, giving him a bear hug. The familiar scent of his pipe floats from his wool cardigan and is comforting.

"Baby girl, it's so good to see you." His twinkling eyes shift to Blake. "Welcome back, son."

"Thanks. It's good to be home."

My father smiles and invites us in. "Why are you two lovebirds hanging at the front door? Come on in already. Blake, your parents are in the kitchen. They're eager to see you."

Blake takes our two bags—my SpongeBob luggage—swinging the duffle over his shoulder and wheeling the roller bag—and ushers me in, his free hand pressed against the small of my back. A tingle shoots through me. How I love the way he tenderly touches me!

Five minutes later, we're all gathered in the kitchen around the island. Blake and I . . . both sets of parents . . . as well as Blake's grandma and her husband Luigi, who will be celebrating their tenth anniversary in

July. They're both now in their early nineties but as sprite as elves. And as sexed as bunnies. Hugs and kisses all around. My heart swells with happiness.

Home! Family! This *is* paradise.

Grandma: "Blakela, so, tell me, did you do a lot of *shtupping?*"

Shtupping means "fucking" in Yiddish. I feel myself flush.

"Mother!" reprimands Blake's mother Helen as she saunters toward the refrigerator.

"Oh yeah, Grandma," replies my husband, stopping her short. His eyes glint fiendishly.

I feel myself heat further. My cheeks are on fire.

"How are the kids?" I ask, quickly changing the subject. I'm eager to see them.

"They're great," says Blake's father. "We all kept them busy."

"Were they worried about us?"

"*Vorried shmorried.*" Grandma flicks her wrist dismissively.

"I taught those little *bambinos* how to play rummy," adds in Luigi. "They beat me every time."

"Thanks, everyone." I laugh. "I was the one who was worried *shmorried.*"

On my next blink, Blake's mother's breathy voice sounds again my ears. "Happy Birthday, darling!"

All eyes turn toward her. She's heading our way, holding a large silver tray with a humongous lit up birthday cake, a bottle of champagne, and some flutes.

Blake's face reddens. He looks so adorable. "Mom! You shouldn't have."

"Of course, I should have. When I heard you were coming home today, I immediately called Hansen's to order your favorite cake." She sets down the tray and everyone breaks into a round of "Happy Birthday."

"Make a wish, darling."

"I wish the kids were with us."

"Darling, they're sound asleep, but I'm sure they'll be up early."

Popping open the champagne, Blake's father gets in a word. "I told them they can have cake for breakfast."

While we've instilled the values of respect, hard work, and kindness into our children, Blake's parents as well as mine love to spoil them. Everyone laughs at Blake's father's comment. His mother insists on another wish.

"But, darling, don't tell us what it is."

I watch as Blake closes his eyes. I wonder what he's wishing for. It just better not be the Cessna he's had his eye on. His eyes re-open.

"Now, my son, blow out the candles," breathes Helen. There must be close to forty candles on the elaborate chocolate buttercream cake. Doing as his mother asks, Blake sucks in a gulp of air and then blows it out, extinguishing the multitude of candles in two breaths. Applause and cheers all around.

"Happy Birthday, baby," I whisper in his ear as his mother slices the cake.

And many, many more

Following the birthday celebration, Blake's parents drive home, taking Grandma and Luigi with them. My parents happily retreat to their cottage, a guesthouse in the rear of our property. Blake and I finish the champagne.

I press a kiss on his lips. "Happy Birthday, baby."

He kisses me back. "Happy Anniversary, tiger."

I set my flute down. "Blake, this has been the best day of my life."

He shoots me his dazzling dimpled smile. "Mine too."

"Come on. Let's check on the kids and call it a night."

Taking our shoes off, we head upstairs, glimpsing the massive lit up Christmas tree in the living room. Dozens of brightly wrapped presents are stacked under it. This might be the best Christmas ever.

Blake leads the way, holding my hand. We quietly tiptoe down a long hallway. I notice that one of the recessed lights is out and point it out to Blake.

"I'll call the electrician in the morning."

I mentally roll my eyes. What happened to handy

dandy Boy Scout Blake? It's weird his mother said nothing about the Boy Scout medallion hanging around my neck. In fact, she eyed it strangely. Hmm. Was he really a Boy Scout? Maybe he found the medal in a thrift store and made the whole thing up, including the photo. Interesting that Boy Scout and bullshit share the same initials. B.S.

I let go of these dubious thoughts when we enter our son's room. Now eight years old, Leo, the spitting image of Blake, is fast asleep. His baseball mitt next to him. He's a major Little Leaguer and his team's MVP. The room is filled with baseball memorabilia from the old baseball cards he collects to a signed baseball Blake caught at a Dodgers' game. My doubts about Blake's Boy Scout days creep back into my mind. It's odd Blake's never asked him to become one.

I peck a kiss on Leo's cheek, thankful he doesn't wake up because he's gotten to the age where my fussing over him is embarrassing.

"He's quite the stud," comments Blake.

This time I really roll my eyes. "Seriously, Blake, you've got to teach him about women. About love and commitment."

Just like his father, my son's gorgeous. And cocky. A blue-eyed babe magnet even at the age of eight. Every girl in his class is in love with him. The same at Hebrew School. Last Valentine's Day, he must have gotten over a hundred "be mine" cards.

"Stop worrying, my love. He'll figure things out." Blake takes my hand and leads me out of the room. Next stop: our daughter's room. Maeve.

In contrast to Leo's sports-inspired room, my precious little girl's bedroom is decorated like a princess's. With its pink and white decor, complete with a regal canopy bed. Sleeping on her back, surrounded by her myriad stuffed animals, my darling daughter brings joy to my heart. Just like her brother. Four days from now on Christmas Day, she will turn five. I'm so grateful Blake and I are alive and here to celebrate her birthday with our entire family.

Holding hands, Blake and I both bend down to give her a chaste kiss on her forehead. She stirs. Then blinks open her eyes. On account of her nightlight, she sees us.

"Mommy! Daddy! You're home!"

"Yes, my darling, we are."

"Can I have birthday cake for breakfast?"

"Of course, you can, princess!" says Blake.

"Did you bring me back a present?"

"Yes," I respond. "Lots!"

Without another word, her eyes close. A smile curled on her rosebud lips, I give her another kiss.

"We're so blessed," I whisper to Blake.

"Yeah, babe, we are."

He takes my hand again.

"C'mon, tiger. Let's finish what we started on the island. I still want to hear you roar."

Epilogue

Blake

ONE YEAR LATER

Oh, yeah! This is gonna be good! This day has already been bitchin.' It started off with a birthday blowjob from my wife, followed by bagels and lox for breakfast with my family. The kids made me birthday cards and showered me with gifts. Leo gave me a drone I can fly with him and Maeve gave me an Easy Bake Oven so she could make me a birthday cake. You gotta love them! My wife gave me a new shirt and tie with a card that read: *You can always use another. Dot. Dot. Dot.* And a P.S. *The rest of your present will come tonight.* She underlined the word "come." Man, I love her and can't wait.

With an unlit cigar dangling from my mouth, I push a button and watch the garage door lower. I'm not talking about the three-car one adjacent to our house. But rather the one under the deluxe RV that sits parked in front of our Santa Monica digs. My newest boy toy.

A birthday present to myself. With a state-of-the art kitchen, a media room, two luxury bathrooms, ours featuring a Jacuzzi tub and steam shower, enough room to sleep eight, a full gym with duo treadmills, and yup, a built-in garage that can house my Porsche, our sleek custom-designed camper cost more than what some houses cost in LA. Jen let me have it on one condition—that I give up flying. After last year's disastrous trip to the Maldives, that wasn't too hard to do though sometimes I do have the urge to sneak away to the Santa Monica airport and take one of those twin-engine Cessnas up for a spin.

From behind me, I hear footsteps and chatter.

"I get the bigger bedroom because I'm older," Leo argues.

"No, I do," counters his soon-to-be six sister Maeve. "Because I'm a girl and I'm prettier. And besides it's my birthday in a couple of days."

"You don't have a *shmekel!*"

"*Shmekel Deckel!*"

My kids are spending way too much time with their loose-lipped grandma. She adores them as they do her. With a chuckle, I look over my shoulder. My wife of eleven years is ambling toward us, pushing our six-month-old twins in a double stroller. Ethan and Emery. True to the promise we made on the island, we decided to adopt another baby. Except we got two for the price of one. A boy and a girl. Very few couples wanted to take on the responsibility of twins, but we jumped at the chance when the opportunity presented itself. Their names respectively mean strong and brave. Fitting after surviving our harrowing ordeal in the Maldives. They're the best babies in the world, and I love them as much as I love Leo and Maeve. Jen feels the same way. And our older children adore their new siblings.

They continue to bicker. Kids! I remember fighting with my sister all the time at that age. It drove my parents crazy. Jen and I have managed to handle it with grace. And authority.

"Kids, stop fighting," I hear Jen say. "We'll flip a coin to see who gets which room." While I can tell Leo, who always wants to get his way—wonder who he gets that from?—is not pleased from the roll of his eyes— my tiger silences them.

"Happy Anniversary, baby!" Spinning around, I beam as she approaches me. I make eye contact with the twins, who are sitting side by side in their stroller. "Ready to go *glamping*, guys?"

It takes very little to make my little ones smile. Their smiles and coos turn my bones into goo. Time after time.

Jen looks worried. "Blake, I'm not sure about this."

"Tiger, relax. We're going to have a blast."

For our first road trip, we're going up to Santa Barbara. To the glamorous camping grounds my parents used to take Marcy and me when we were kids. Along with all the creature comforts this RV has to offer, including the ability to take my Porsche for a drive if my need for speed strikes, we won't be wanting for much. Only an hour and a half away, I thought our destination would make for the perfect maiden voyage of the *Thatmobile*.

Yup, that's what I've decided to name my vehicle. Batman has his Batmobile. This superhero—*That Man*—has his Thatmobile. Leo thinks it's pretty lame. Maeve loves it. When I told her I was a superhero, she laughed. "Daddy, you can't fly." Jen immediately jumped in. "Sweetie, you're absolutely right. Daddy *can't* fly." Reminding me again that flying planes is off limits.

I help Jen get the twins into their car seats. We've had the extravagant caravan custom-fitted to include age-appropriate safety constraints for all the passengers. Wherever they are in the vehicle, they'll be protected in case of an accident. "Of course, we won't have one," I assured my worried wife. To which she replied: "Says the man who almost crash landed a plane." I don't think she'll ever stop reminding me.

After folding up the stroller and packing it into the vehicle—I swear, with all the stuff we've brought along for our three-day outing, the storage area of the RV looks like the inside of a Target—I watch Leo and Maeve clamber in.

"This is so cool, Daddy! It's like a house on

wheels!" exclaims my princess as they both gallop to the media room. My wife follows them to make sure they're buckled in properly.

"All's good," she says when she returns, climbing into the passenger seat in the front of the RV next to mine. "What's even better, I got them to agree on watching a movie on the big screen TV."

"What are they watching?"

"*Are We There Yet?*"

"Perfect." My mind flashes back to last year at about this time when my wife asked me that very question just before we were forced to make an emergency landing in the middle of the Indian Ocean. I inwardly shudder at the memory of the plane going down. Nope, that wasn't fun. We've never told the kids about our near-death experience. We may never. There's no reason for them to know.

With all the horrors of that trip behind us, we can finally laugh about it. Well, let me rephrase, parts of it. Every time we think about our rescue in the middle of fucking our brains out—Jen naked with her hands tied behind her back and me with my gigantic erection that I had to cover up with my shirt—we burst into laughter. Sometimes, we laugh until we cry. You have to admit, that was pretty funny, and it could *only* happen to us. That Man and Calamity Jen. My cock, Mr. Burns, will never let me live that one down. No pun intended. Tonight, after the kids are fast asleep, he's going to help me christen this baby. Yup, in honor of our eleventh anniversary, I'm going to fuck my tiger senseless on our luxurious king-size bed. I may even break open her new battery-operated sex toy—one of our Christmas traditions. And break it in.

As Jen fastens her seatbelt, I close the passenger door. I jog around the RV and hop into my plush leather seat. Man, it actually feels better than being in the pilot's seat of a Gulfstream 650. The roomy chair even pivots as does Jen's. I push the ignition and start up the million-dollar vehicle. The diesel engine purrs. Oh, yeah! This is *definitely* gonna be good!

"Ready for our next adventure, baby?"

"Every minute of the day is an adventure with you, Blake."

That's for sure. I can't deny it. I pull away from the curb.

"Away we go!" I pick up speed as we cruise to the nearby Coast Highway. I frickin' love this thing.

"Blake, we've got precious cargo in this vehicle. I want you to keep your eyes on the road and both hands on the wheel. And no speeding. Or distractions."

"Aww, baby, you're taking all the fun away. Can't I even put my hand on your thigh?" Stretching my arm, I set my hand on her leg, dangerously close to her pussy.

"Fine. Only if you promise you won't ask me to drive this monster."

"Deal." I don't tell her we can put this baby into

auto drive, a feature I may need to use later. Flexing, Mr. Burns agrees as she questions me.

"You swear?"

I wink at her.

"Scout's Honor."

A LETTER FROM BLAKE

Hey there, all you beautiful and sexy readers~ Well, my tiger and I made it through ten years of marriage. Actually, eleven. Let me tell you, though, there were way more than a couple of times I thought we wouldn't. Jen and I have been through a lot together, but it's made us only closer. Stronger. I hate to think of what would have happened if the Coast Guard hadn't found us on that remote island in the Maldives.

Sometimes, my tiger has nightmares of still being there. Our skin fried. Our bodies wasting away from malnutrition. Fighting disease and battling the forces of nature. And there's another nightmare she's shared with me . . . of us finally being found thirty-five years later. Me, at the age of seventy-five. Her not far behind me at sixty-nine. Coming home to find our parents long gone, all our kids married with grown kids of their own and moving on.

But that's not what happened or ever will. My wise old man once told me there are patterns in life. Patterns that repeat themselves. Some people continue to fall down; others fall up. Ours is to succeed. To survive no matter what life brings us. Often I think that fate put us on that island to test our love and our strength. Our commitment to one another.

I learned a lot about myself on that island. First and foremost, that I'm not really Superman. I don't really have superpowers. It's my tiger, who gives me strength and my need to protect those I love. She makes me a better person. Without her, I'd be a shell of the man that I am. Without her, I don't know how I'd go on. Keep this a secret between "us girls." I want my tiger to think that I'm invincible—that'll always come through for her and our family. I want to believe this too.

In less than ten years, I'll be frickin' fifty. But you know what? I'll still look like that scorchin' hot dude on the cover of this book. Yup, *That Man.* And I'll still be with my beautiful tiger. Loving and fucking her like there's no tomorrow. I can't wait to see what life brings us over the next decade. Especially with our kids as we watch them grow up. There's no doubt in my mind that Leo, the lion, will be running Conquest Broadcasting one day, and my beautiful little princess Maeve will be ruling the world. Madam President. She's something else. Just like her mom. As for the twins, it's too early to tell, but the world is their oyster.

Want to know what I wished for on my fortieth birthday? I'll tell you. Yeah, I could have wished for a lot of toys from my long list. And a blowjob. But I didn't. What I wished for wasn't too original, but after our near-death experience in the Maldives, I wished for happiness, love, good health, and longevity for my entire family. Selfless of me, right? Good things happen to good people. Just so happens I got a mind-blowing blowjob anyway from my talented wife and a lot more.

While I'm sure you're smiling—and I love all your smiles—I bet there's one thing that's driving you crazy. Was I really a Boy Scout? Sorry, my beauties, I'm not going to tell you; you'll have to ask my mother. Good luck! I've sworn her to secrecy.

Until next time, **I T**otally. **A**lways. **L**ove. **Y**ou. Thanks, my beauties, for sharing our story.

I.T.A.L.Y.~xo Blake

POSTSCRIPT

SIX WEEKS LATER
Azheeckal, India

T he sun is blazing, the white sand shimmering, the turquoise ocean ebbing and flowing. One would never know by looking at this breathtaking, tranquil scene that a monstrous monsoon had ravaged the little coastal village just a few weeks ago. A disaster. Today, it's picture postcard perfect. A good day to fish.

The fisherman has brought along his family. Lucky for him, the ruthless tropical storm with its massive downpour, gusting winds, and raging waves spared his hut along with his wife and child. Many died; others suffered injuries, and some like his neighbor lost everything, including his wife and home. The man feels blessed.

While he casts his homemade fishing pole into the sea, his six-year-old son frolics in the gentle waves. His wife, dressed in a traditional sari, sits on the beach close by on a woven straw mat, shaving the husk of a coconut to make yarn. She keeps a watchful eye on her beloved little boy, admiring his sugar-brown skin, glossy raven hair, and his slight but athletic body. The beautiful boy that will someday grow up to be a handsome man. The boy that she hopes will someday go to University and live a different life than hers and her husband's. Work in a big city at a big job instead of peddling fish and wares in their small seaside village.

Something catches the attention of the little boy. The fisherman and his wife see it too. No, it's not a big catch, but rather, a piece of luggage.

"Look, Papa!" shouts the little boy. Excitedly, he runs toward the object, making splashes in his wake.

"Careful, Samar!" calls out his concerned mother.

Ignoring her words, he continues to gallop toward the suitcase, the water waist-deep, and retrieves it, clutching the handle. The suitcase is heavy, and it is a struggle for the slender child to haul it to shore. But he is strong and determined. When he reaches the coast, his father takes it from him and sets it on the beach.

"LV," says the little boy, studying the large soaked bag, showing off to his parents that he can read English. His vigilant mother smiles as she knows English will be important for him to succeed. She and her husband can also speak and read this universal language, thanks to taking a course at a local mission.

"What do you think is inside?" asks the child.

"Let's find out," responds his father, setting down his pole.

As his son and wife eagerly look on, the man, who is unusually tall and athletically built, unzips the case. His eyes grow wide at the contents.

It's a suitcase full of Western clothing. A man's. While the items are drenched from being submerged in the sea, he can tell they are expensive. The kind of stylish clothes the rich American and British tourists wear. Among them, designer jeans, T-shirts, sweaters, shorts, bathing trunks, Italian shoes, and even a fancy jacket. He randomly takes out one of the many pair of jeans and holds them against him.

"Rahul," says the wife. "They look like they will fit you."

The man smiles. He knows they will.

"Is there anything for me?" shouts the little boy. On his next breath, he rummages through the suitcase. His big brown eyes light up.

"Look! A baseball cap." He reads the embroidered logo on the front of it. "LA Dodgers. Cool!" A sports buff, he knows about the Dodgers from his computer at school. Not wasting time, he puts on the hat, and though it's way too big for him, he looks adorable. His mother beams.

Hoping to find more booty, the little boy continues to riffle through the bag. He finds a framed photo and shows it to his parents. It's a picture of a boy about his age, maybe a little older, being awarded a medal.

"Maybe this is the man's son," says the father.

As the little boy digs deeper, a pang of sadness shoots through the woman. Perhaps this man was shipwrecked. Or in a plane crash. Lost at sea during the terrible storm. She mourns silently for him. For his wife. And his child.

Her sad thoughts are interrupted by her son's sweet voice. "Look, Mama, at what else I found." He holds up a glass object that's filled with water and shakes it. Tiny particles of glitter dance about in the crystal-clear liquid inside it. While he's never seen them, the particles remind him of snowflakes.

"Here, Mama. This is for you."

With a melancholy smile, the woman takes the object from her son. She knows what it is. At the market, there is a vendor who sells similar ones with a miniature statue of the Taj Mahal inside. A snow globe.

Mesmerized by the sparkly flakes, she shakes the globe again. This time, two shimmering objects inside the globe come into view. She gasps. They look like a pair of diamond earrings, each one resembling a snowflake. Carefully, she removes the bottom of the globe. The water pours out as the earrings fall into the palm of her hand. Her eyes grow wide as the pair of platinum and diamond earrings capture the sunlight and shimmer in her eyes.

"Oh my goodness, these are beautiful," she says softly.

"Let me put them on you," says her husband.

Though she's not wearing her usual dangling earrings, her ears are pierced and have been since she was a child. Trembling a little, she lets the man she has loved all her life put them on her. His touch is gentle as he secures them with the posts. They hang from her ears like two dancing snowflakes. She puts her fingers to them in awe, eager to see what they look like on her lobes. Her husband for now is her mirror.

"Anaya, they look beautiful on you. They are meant to be yours."

Cosmic treasures.

Before she can respond, her little boy's voice captures her attention. "Look, Mama, there's a note." He holds up an envelope and then hands it to his mother.

Carefully, she opens it. The paper is soggy and fragile. Inside it is a card engraved with silver-foiled, flowery letters. She reads it out loud.

"Happy Tenth Anniversary, My Wife."

Ironically or not, today's her tenth anniversary wedded to Rahul. The kind, handsome man she loves with her body, heart, and soul. Teary-eyed, she flips open the card. Inside is a poem. Her voice thin and watery, she reads aloud again.

> Tiger, tiger burning bright
> In the shadows of the night.
> I love you up close
> And shining from afar.

You're my beautiful shining star.

You give me direction; you give me light.

Let me be your shining knight.

I promise to cherish you from this day on

Until death do us part, whatever our plight.

Let me be your hero and you'll be my shrine;

I'll worship you even when I'm gone.

Eternal love; eternal might,

My heart is forever yours; Yours forever mine.

Her voice grows more and more watery as she reads it. And by the end, tears are trickling down her cheeks. Knowing how much this man, whose washed-away handwritten name she can't read, loved his wife, a sadness so profound sweeps over her that it hurts her heart to breathe. Her intuitive, loving husband squeezes her free hand.

"Mama, are you okay?" asks her concerned little boy.

She nods. "Yes, my darling."

She gazes into the horizon, watching the sun, a great ball of fire, sink into the sea. Thinking of all the things that were and could have been. And maybe, just maybe, can still be if they're meant to.

She experiences an almost out-of-body, soulful connection to the past, the present, and the future. An all-consuming ray of light fleets through her being.

Having once lost a child, she knows of both dreams and despair, love and remorse. A song of melancholy and hope fills her heart as she beholds her precious boy.

"My son, when you grow up, I hope you will become *that* man."

A NOTE FROM NELLE

My Dearest Belle Readers~

Thank you SO much for reading THAT MAN 6. I hope you loved reading it as much as I loved writing it. It was so much fun to write about scorchin' hot Blake Burns again! If you did enjoy it, I hope you will write a review. It can be as long or short as you wish. It would mean so much to me as reviews help others find my books.

Do you want more of scorchin' hot Blake Burns? He and his tiger Jen are featured in my UNFORGETTA-BLE trilogy (also available as a Box Set) and my romantic comedy standalone, BABY DADDY. Check out these hot and hilarious romantic comedies on my website!

UNFORGETTABLE

BABY DADDY

If you want to read a sampling of my books, please check out my romance compilation.

NAUGHTY NELLE

Exciting news! I plan to bring you more books soon. REMEMBER ME, a steamy, suspenseful romance ripped from the headlines, and my "mystery book," a brand new standalone romantic comedy, will be published in Fall 2018. Add them to your Goodreads TBR list!

REMEMBER ME
MYSTERY ROMCOM

Please follow me on social media to learn about my releases, sales, and giveaways. Always feel free to contact me. I LOVE hearing from my readers and I always reply personally. Again, thank you from the bottom of my heart for your love and support! You are the reason I write!

MWAH! ~ Nelle ♥

ACKNOWLEDGMENTS

First and foremost, thank you all my belles readers for embracing THAT MAN Blake Burns and his tiger. And for keeping his naughty, loveable spirit alive.

More thanks goes to the following:

My Bestest Betas: Angie Birkle, Debra DeBruin Brzoska, Marti Jentis, Wanda Kather, Dawn Myers, Kristen Myers, Mary Jo Toth, and Joanne Warren. Your insightful comments were invaluable!

My Aviation Guru: Joe "the stud" Warren. I hope one day you'll take me flying!

My Personal Assistant: Keyanna Butler. You've been a godsend!

My Amazing Cover Artist: Arijana Karčic/Cover It! Designs. I'm beholden to you for creating among the most iconic book covers ever! I'm running out of colors!

My Patient Formatter: Paul Salvette/BB eBooks. Thank you once again for putting up with all my craziness. One of these days I'll get it right the first time around!

My Eagle Eye Proofreader: Mary Jo Toth. I adore you!

My Release Blitz Organizer Give Me Books: Thank you Kylie, Jo, and Lucy for always being there for me.

All the Amazing Bloggers: A big shout out for tirelessly promoting and reviewing my books and for all you do for indie authors.

All my ARC Readers: Thank you for wanting to read THAT MAN 6 and voluntarily writing your amazing reviews. I will read every one of them!

Last but not least . . .

A big thank you to my family for putting up with me. And my fur baby Pepper for your always being by my side and loving me unconditionally.

LOVE you all!

MWAH! ~ Nelle ♥

ABOUT THE AUTHOR

Nelle L'Amour is a *New York Times* and *USA Today* bestselling author who lives in Los Angeles with her Prince Charming-ish husband, twin princesses, and a bevy of royal pain-in-the-butt pets. A former executive in the entertainment industry with a prestigious Humanitas Prize for promoting human dignity and freedom to her credit, she gave up playing with Barbies a long time ago, but still enjoys playing with toys with her husband. While she writes in her PJs, she loves to get dressed up and pretend she's Hollywood royalty. Her steamy stories feature characters that will make you laugh, cry, and swoon and stay in your heart forever.

To learn about her new releases, sales, and giveaways, please sign up for her newsletter and follow her on social media. Nelle loves to hear from her readers.

Check out her cool website:
www.nellelamour.com

Sign up for her fun newsletter:
nellelamour.com/newsletter

Join her FB Reader Group: Nelle's Belles:
facebook.com/groups/1943750875863015

Follow her on Bookbub:
bookbub.com/authors/nelle-l-amour

Join her Facebook Fan Page
facebook.com/NelleLamourAuthor

Follow her on Twitter:
twitter.com/nellelamour

Email her at:
nellelamour@gmail.com

Follow her on Amazon:
amazon.com/Nelle-LAmour/e/B00ATHR0LQ

BOOKS BY NELLE L'AMOUR

Unforgettable
Unforgettable Book 1
Unforgettable Book 2
Unforgettable Book 3

Alpha Billionaire Duet
TRAINWRECK 1
TRAINWRECK 2

A Standalone Romantic Comedy
Baby Daddy

An OTT Insta-love Standalone
The Big O

THAT MAN Series
THAT MAN 1
THAT MAN 2
THAT MAN 3
THAT MAN 4
THAT MAN 5
THAT MAN 6

Gloria
Gloria's Secret
Gloria's Revenge
Gloria's Forever

An Erotic Love Story
Undying Love
Endless Love

Writing as E.L. Sarnoff
DEWITCHED: The Untold Story of the Evil Queen
UNHITCHED: The Untold Story of the Evil Queen 2

Boxed Sets
THAT MAN TRILOGY
THAT MAN: THE WEDDING STORY
Unforgettable: The Complete Series
Gloria's Secret: The Trilogy
Seduced by the Park Avenue Billionaire
Naughty Nelle

16378121R00099

Printed in Great Britain
by Amazon